The Diary of
Laura's Twin

Kathy Kacer

Second Story Press

Library and Archives Canada Cataloguing in Publication

Kacer, Kathy, 1954-

The diary of Laura's twin / by Kathy Kacer.

(Holocaust remembrance series for young readers)

ISBN 978-1-897187-39-5

1. Holocaust, Jewish (1939-1945—Poland—Warsaw—Juvenile fiction. 2. Jewish
children in the Holocaust—Poland—Warsaw—Juvenile fiction. 3. Bat mitzvah—Juvenile
fiction. I. Title. II. Series: Holocaust remembrance book for young readers

PS8571.A33D52 2008   jC813'.54   C2007-906433-7

Edited by Peter Carver
Cover and text design by Melissa Kaita
Printed and bound in Canada

*The views or opinons expressed in this book and the context in which the images are used,
do not necessarily reflect the views or policy of, nor imply approval or endorsement by,
the United States Holocaust Memorial Museum.*

*Second Story Press gratefully acknowledges the support of the Ontario Arts Council and the
Canada Council for the Arts for our publishing program. We acknowledge the financial support of
the Government of Canada through the Book Publishing Industry Development Program.*

ONTARIO ARTS COUNCIL
CONSEIL DES ARTS DE L'ONTARIO

Canada Council   Conseil des Arts
for the Arts   du Canada

Published by
SECOND STORY PRESS
20 Maud Street, Suite 401
Toronto, Ontario, Canada
M5V 2M5
www.secondstorypress.ca

To Gabby Samra and Dexter Glied-Beliak,
for keeping the memory alive.

Prologue

January 10, 1943

My name is Sara Gittler and I am thirteen and a half years old. I have lived here in the Warsaw Ghetto for more than a year. Can you imagine what it is like to live behind barbed wire and high walls? No one can leave and no one wants to come in. There are thousands of Jews, just like me, who are living here — if you can call it that. But this is not really living. To me, living means that you are free; that you can go where you want and do anything you wish. We are anything but free. I can't go to school, there are no parks for me to play in, I have so little to eat that I am starving all the time. Maybe what I mean to say is that we exist here — my family and I, and the other Jews. We are in limbo, praying for things to get better, expecting that things will get worse.

I once read a story about a bird that was caged up for years until someone came along and set it free. It spread its wings and lifted up into the sky, floating on a current of air, loving the sweet moment of its liberation. But unbeknownst to the bird, a hungry cat had been watching from behind a tree. Within seconds, the cat leapt into the sky, caught the bird, and killed it. Now you'd think that the saddest part of that story was that the bird died. But that's not the part that made me sad. The part that made me sad was that the bird was caged up in the first place.

I dream of walking down a busy street and stopping in a café for ice cream and cake. I dream of going to a real school and sitting at the front of the classroom where I can listen to every word the teacher says. I dream of buying a new dress, or maybe ten of them. Most of all, I dream of being a famous writer and having everyone read my stories and remember my name. I have written dozens of stories and they are all here in this diary. They tell of my life in the ghetto, along with the lives of my family members and best friends. This is my childhood. I don't deserve to be here. I did nothing wrong. My only crime is that I was born Jewish and for that, I have been imprisoned and condemned.

If you are reading my stories, it means you found them in the special place I am leaving them. And that means that I am not here to read them with you, to tell you about my life, and to share the memories. My stories speak for my life; they speak for me. Please, remember me.

Sara Gittler

Chapter One

It was scary to hear everyone remind her that she was becoming an adult.

"You're all grown up now," her mother said, looking thoughtful and a little sad.

"You realize that as an adult you'll be more responsible for your actions," her father would add, more seriously.

It was all so overwhelming. Not that she didn't look forward to milestones — those special events that were markers in her life — like seasons or birthdays, only better and more important. At the age of sixteen she would be able to drive, at eighteen she could vote. But at the age of twelve, Laura Wyman was about to celebrate her Bat Mitzvah — the coming of age ceremony for Jewish girls.

What does it really mean to come of age? Laura wondered. It was nice to have more freedom with each passing year. She could use the subway more often and go to the mall without having to check in with her mother every hour! But there had to be more to this moment in her life than subways and malls. It was as if everyone expected her Bat Mitzvah to be this magic moment when everything she had done up to that point was just practice for adulthood and everything from then on would be real. Was she going to wake up the day after her celebration and look and feel completely different? Good-bye, Laura the child, and hello, young woman! It was serious stuff, starting with the ceremony.

First, there would be a service in her synagogue. Laura would stand on the podium and read from the Torah, the Hebrew scroll of biblical writings. But after that, it would be party time. Everyone from her class was going to be there, along with her cousins, aunts and uncles, family friends, and those important "business" associates her father always referred to. Laura didn't really think too much about any of her parents' friends; they could invite whoever they wanted. She cared about her family, and she cared that her school friends were going to have the best time ever. There was going to be a DJ and lots of giveaways — sports items and other party favors that would be awarded to the best dancers. Laura expected that she would receive some amazing gifts.

All this was happening in less than a month. But first, Laura had to make it through the Hebrew classes that would prepare her for the synagogue service. Along with the other boys and girls who were studying for their Bar and Bat Mitzvahs, Laura had been attending those classes twice a week after school for a full year; there was a lot to learn if you were preparing to become an adult! That's where Laura was right now, struggling to stay awake and counting the minutes until the class was over and she could finally go home. The rabbi was talking, and Laura put aside her papers and tried to pay attention.

"I have a very important assignment to tell you about," the rabbi began. "It means some extra work, but I assure you the work is meaningful. It will add so much to your Bar and Bat Mitzvah experience."

Laura couldn't believe what she was hearing. Another assignment? Impossible! She had too much to do already. There was that geography project she still had to finish at school, and another novel to read for a book report. Oh, and she couldn't forget the science test that was scheduled for two weeks from today. That was just the classroom work. Then there was her volleyball team — the finals were coming up in a few weeks which meant she would be practicing three times a week instead of just twice. Plus, Laura had promised her mother that she would babysit her five-year-old sister, Emma, this weekend. Laura had so much already on her plate, let alone having to do extra work here for her Bat Mitzvah class.

The thought of everything she had to do was enough to make Laura groan out loud. A boy sitting in front of her turned to glance curiously in her direction. "Hey, are you sick?" Laura felt her face go hot with embarrassment. His name was Daniel and he was cute — dark eyes and a really nice smile. Normally, Laura would have liked the attention, but at this moment she wished he would look away. She shook her head. Sick? No. Desperate? Yes!

"We are developing a new project here at our synagogue — a twinning project," the rabbi was saying. "What that means is that each one of you will begin to learn something about a child your age who perished during the Holocaust. Many of you know that of the six million Jewish people who died or were killed in the Holocaust, one and a half million were children. Many of those children never had the opportunity to celebrate their Bar or Bat Mitzvah as you are doing now. You will have the chance, through our twinning project, to do it on their behalf."

Laura shifted in her seat and closed her eyes, trying to take some deep breaths. It was one thing to spend the time learning Hebrew for the prayers she would need to recite in the synagogue. The truth was that part wasn't hard for Laura. She learned quickly, and she loved deciphering the Hebrew letters and words; it was like trying to decode a secret language. Her parents worried about how she would do with the Hebrew, but Laura knew she'd be fine with that part. But now the rabbi was asking for something more to add to her already hectic schedule.

"Now then, I'm sure you are all wondering what this will involve, so let me try and explain this to you." The rabbi continued talking. He said that every child in the class would have to research a boy or girl their age who had lived during the time of World War II and the Holocaust, the 1930s and 40s. They'd have to find out who the child was, learn about their family and where they were during the war, *and* what happened to them all. He said that these children could be family members, or relatives of someone from the synagogue or from the community.

"There are also those who survived the Holocaust and are still alive today who never had the chance to have a real Bar or Bat Mitzvah when they were young," the rabbi continued. "You might even think about contacting one of these survivors and seeing if they might be interested in participating with you in the twinning project." Each student in Laura's class would have the opportunity to give a speech about their Holocaust child on the day of their own Bar or Bat Mitzvah — to remember them in some way that was meaningful. "It is a privilege to celebrate your coming of age, and it is a blessing to share that day with a child who never had the opportunities that each one of you has," the rabbi concluded as he handed out a package of information about the twinning program. "This project can enhance your own ceremony and make it even more meaningful. I hope you take it seriously, and I'm here to help if anyone needs more information."

Laura wanted her Bat Mitzvah to be personal and meaningful, not just a big party, though she certainly intended for that part to be fun. She had spent a long time thinking about what this event really meant to her, and she wanted to do something that showed she was serious about it. That was when the idea of raising money for Africa had come to her. She had read about how important clean drinking water was for people in Africa. Children contracted horrible diseases from dirty water. Women and children often spent hours every day walking back and forth from their homes to the few wells where the water was safe to drink. Laura had decided that one way she could do something important would be to raise money that she would send to the African Well Fund. She was excited by the project and spent almost every day after school going door to door collecting money in her neighborhood and beyond. After two months Laura had raised almost $1,000. She sent the money to the African organization knowing in her heart that she had done something worthwhile. She even received a letter of thanks from some children in Africa, which she had framed and hung on her bedroom wall. That's what her Bat Mitzvah meant to her. It was about looking forward and seeing how she could contribute to her community, not looking back. You can't change the stuff that happened in the past, Laura thought. But you can change the future.

Besides, Laura already knew a lot about the Holocaust. She had done a project on it the year before for her grade six class. The project was hard. Every time Laura had to read about someone who had been killed in the war, her stomach lurched and she could barely finish. It was too much to think that there were children who would never experience happy events, or have the things she was lucky to have. Laura had finished the project — barely — and that was enough. In Laura's mind there wasn't anything else to learn. How is researching one more child who died going to add anything to my own Bat Mitzvah? she wondered. The war was ancient history as far as Laura was concerned.

Maybe she could have her parents call the rabbi and explain to him that she had already completed an important community project by fund-raising for the well *and* that she had too little time to undertake yet another assignment. But a part of Laura didn't want this to get to her parents. Deep down she knew they would think it was a wonderful idea. And worse, they might make it even bigger than it was already — insisting that she do extra research, contact more people, write letters to museums. The thought of what her parents might do with this was making Laura panic. No, it was better not to involve them. She had to deal with this alone. And the first step was to try and talk to the rabbi.

The class was ending. Laura shoved her papers quickly into her backpack and approached the rabbi at the front of the room. "Excuse me, Rabbi Gardiner?" The rabbi was gathering his books. He paused, perched himself on the edge of his desk and removed his glasses. "I think I'm going to have a problem with this project," Laura began. "You see, it's just that I have so much work to do right now, and my Bat Mitzvah is only three weeks away. I'm very busy — too busy to take on anything else." She sounded lame — and whiny — even to her own ears. Okay, she thought desperately. This approach isn't working. I've got to try something else. Laura took a deep breath and continued. "I made a choice with my parents about what kind of project I was going to do for my Bat Mitzvah." That sounds better, she thought. A choice sounded more grown-up. "That's why I raised money for Africa. Besides," she added. "I don't know anyone who's been through the Holocaust — not personally." Laura's parents were born in Canada; her

9

grandparents had been born here as well. There were distant relatives — she didn't know them — who came from Russia or some other country like that. But that was centuries ago. Well, maybe not quite centuries, but a really long time back. Laura had no personal ties to the Holocaust, just the history that she had learned about. "So you see, while I think it's very important to remember the Holocaust, I just don't think this project is for me." Her voice trailed off and she stood meekly in front of the rabbi.

Surely he would understand her situation. He was a reasonable man. In fact, Rabbi Gardiner was pretty cool. He was young, younger than her father, and he even played guitar. He didn't look like those old rabbis she had seen in other synagogues, and nothing like the ones from old photographs with their long flowing white beards and stooped shoulders. Rabbi Gardiner understood young people. He would understand Laura's situation.

The rabbi was gazing at her attentively, his head tilted to one side. Finally, he replaced his glasses, reached for a piece of paper on his desk, looked at it for a moment, and then looked up at Laura. "I understand what you're saying," he said. "And I don't want you to think that I don't appreciate how busy you are, or how much work you've already done. But I want you to do me one favor." Laura waited expectantly while the rabbi continued. "There is a woman whom I would like you to contact. Her name and telephone number are on this piece of paper."

"Who is she?" asked Laura as she accepted the paper that the rabbi held out in front of him.

"She's a very interesting person — an elderly woman who might be able to give you a new perspective on this. I'd like you to go and visit her. Just once," he added. "If you're not interested in pursuing this after one visit, then I'll understand. But promise me, you'll go once, and you'll listen to what she has to say."

Laura looked down at the paper she held in her hand, and then back up at the rabbi. She hated mysteries and the rabbi was being particularly mystifying.

"She'll be expecting your call. Will you go?"

Laura sighed. No harm in one visit. That much she could handle. She nodded, slung her backpack over her shoulder, and headed out the door.

Chapter Two

"So, explain this 'twinning' thing to me again. It's not like you actually had a twin sister in World War II. This isn't some weird life-after-death experience, is it?"

Laura was walking to school with her best friend, Nix — Nicole Wilcox. They had known each other for years, since kindergarten classes, but had only become close this year in grade seven. That first day in this new school had been a nightmare for Laura, and when she couldn't find her way through the maze of corridors and staircases to her first class, it was Nix who had come to her rescue.

"The trick is to follow a grade nine student and look like you belong. It's all in the attitude," Nix had said confidently as she grabbed Laura's arm and steered her in the right direction. That had sealed their friendship, and since that first day, the two girls had become inseparable. Nix was tall, blond, and pretty — everyone thought so — with sparkling gray-blue eyes. And next to Laura with her straight dark hair and dark brown eyes, Nix was the complete opposite. She was athletic, while Laura was studious; she was outspoken and boisterous, while Laura was quiet and shy. But as friends, they fit together perfectly, complementing each other's personalities. "You're like peanut butter and jam," Laura's father often joked. "Okay on your own, but an even better combination."

"Of course it's not weird," sighed Laura, checking her watch to make sure they were not going to be late for class. She had a thing about being on time, which also drove Nix — who was perpetually late — crazy! "It's not an actual blood twin. It's just a way of remembering someone who died during the war."

Nix nodded. "That veteran came to talk to us last year about how he fought in World War II. He got some kind of medal for being part of the landing at Normandy in France. He said he was away from his home and his family for more than a year. But it was so romantic, remember? He said he always knew he'd come back to his wife, even though it was dangerous and he was being shot at all the time." Nix threw her head back in a dramatic pose.

"Right," said Laura. "Except that I'm talking about Jewish *children* who were in the war — nothing romantic about it. They never had a chance to fight — neither did their parents. Most of them were killed."

Nix's family was Anglican. Sometimes Laura felt as if she had to explain the basics of Jewish history and religion to her friend. Then again, Nix usually had to teach her all about Anglican practices, too. The first time Laura had ever set foot in a church was when she had gone to midnight mass with Nix's family this past Christmas. The church was dark except for the dozens of candles that cast golden shadows across the pews and pulpit. It was beautiful, and when the church service was over, Laura had gone home with Nix to admire their Christmas tree, adorned with silver bells, colorful lights, and strands of tinsel. Mrs. Wilcox explained that some of the ornaments had been in their family for more than fifty years.

"I know what happened during the war," said Nix. "I read *The Diary of Anne Frank* last summer. I hate thinking about what it must have been like for Anne not to be able to walk outside that hiding place for two years. I'd go crazy if I couldn't go out. And I couldn't believe it when the soldiers broke into her hiding place to arrest her whole family. I mean, it was so close to the end of the war, and I really thought that Anne would make it. I nearly cried when I read about what happened to them.

"Hey, do you want to come over after school today? I got this amazing scanner for my computer with a new program that can do almost anything to photos. We can draw mustaches on people!"

Laura gazed at her friend and smiled. She was struck by how simple it was for Nix to talk about Anne Frank in one breath, and computer equipment in the next. "I can't," she said. "I'm supposed to go and visit this old lady who's going to give me some information about the twinning thing." Laura still wasn't sure she was going to go ahead with the project. But last night, just as she had promised the rabbi, she had made a telephone call to Mrs. Mandelcorn, the lady whose name she had been given. Laura had been embarrassed during the call because Mrs. Mandelcorn didn't seem to understand what she was asking. Neither did Laura, really. While her English was quite good, Mrs. Mandelcorn had a heavy accent and Laura had struggled to understand everything that she said. So there were long silences as each waited for the other to speak. Laura felt less and less certain that there was any point to her going to see the woman.

"Come vees-eet me tomorrow, and vee vil tok," Mrs. Mandelcorn had finally said. It was going to be another late evening out instead of doing the things Laura *had* to do. But what choice did she have? A promise was a promise — especially one that was made to a rabbi.

"Where are you going tonight, and how come you didn't invite me?"

Laura and Nix turned as their friend, Adam Segal, approached. If Nix was Laura's closest girlfriend, then Adam was her closest guy friend; more like a brother actually. Laura quickly explained the twinning project to Adam and her upcoming visit with Mrs. Mandelcorn.

"I don't know what to do about it," said Laura. "I've already done a project for my Bat Mitzvah, and I don't have time to work on another one."

"It sounds cool," said Adam, flipping his mop of brown hair off his forehead and adjusting his glasses. He prided himself on the circular blue John Lennon glasses that were his trademark. In fact, Adam was a genius when it came to anything that had to do with the Beatles, a walking encyclopedia of facts and trivia. Where and when every song had been performed, statistics on each member of the group — he knew it all. "I should have been born in the Sixties," he often joked.

"My grandfather was in the Holocaust," Adam said. Laura didn't know that. She glanced up at her friend. "Yeah," he continued, "he was only fifteen when his whole family was sent to a concentration camp. My grandfather was the only one who survived."

Laura didn't want to hear this. "What does that have to do with my visit to Mrs. Mandelcorn?" she asked, checking her watch again impatiently.

"No, listen," continued Adam. "He talks to me all the time about what happened to him and his family. His stories are amazing — and kind of scary."

Was that part of it? Laura wondered. Was she also afraid of delving further into a time in history when life for Jewish people had been so terrifying? The pictures she saw when she was researching her Holocaust project had been enough to make her lose sleep for days. Perhaps her reluctance to do this twinning project was not only that she was busy, not only that she had already completed a community project, not only that her Bat Mitzvah date was looming — but perhaps also that the thought of finding a child her age who had died would sadden and scare her far too much.

Laura shook her head. No, that couldn't be it. She had made a choice about her Bat Mitzvah, she reminded herself. She was working on goals for the future, not dredging up stuff from the past.

Adam wouldn't give up. "My grandfather is always saying how important it is to talk about what happened to Jews during the war."

"Are you not listening?" Laura thought she was going to explode. "I've done my project. It was really interesting, but it was a ton of work. This is different from just talking to someone." Laura glared at Adam. He was beginning to sound like Rabbi Gardiner — or her father. Didn't anyone understand the pressure she was under?

"You've just got to give it a chance," said Adam. "You never know what can happen." He threw back his head and started to sing, "*We all wanna change the world.*" Then he stopped and grinned. "That's what John said."

The bell was about to ring. The pace around the schoolyard was picking up. Crowds of boys and girls were pushing their way through the doors to get to their first class. Adam flashed a peace sign, charged up the stairs and into the building.

"Call me," said Nix. She disappeared into a throng of students pushing to get to class.

Laura watched the commotion for a moment longer. She had to shake this feeling that was weighing her down. Maybe the meeting with the old lady would be fine. Maybe she would ace all of her upcoming tests and assignments. Maybe she'd win a lottery and multiply herself into ten people!

Chapter Three

Laura shifted uncomfortably as her mother continued talking to her on the drive to Mrs. Mandelcorn's place.

"It may be difficult to understand this lady at first, but you'll get used to the way she talks," her mom said. "It's just like my Aunt Yvonne. These days, I hardly notice her German accent at all."

Her mother had insisted that she drive Laura over to the apartment where Mrs. Mandelcorn lived, even though Laura had wanted to take the bus, or ride her bike. A long bike ride would have helped clear her head and prepare her for this meeting. But her mom had not let up. Laura finally gave in.

The less her mother became involved in this project the better, thought Laura again. Not that she wasn't grateful for the things her mom did. Laura's mother was the car pool queen, transporting Laura and her friends whenever and wherever they wanted to go, often rearranging her own schedule to fit theirs. "Sometimes I feel as if I was born with a steering wheel in my hands," she often joked. Laura enjoyed hanging out with her mother. The two of them loved going to those sappy girly movies that her dad never wanted to see. And her mom was great to talk to — usually — just as long as she didn't get over involved in things. And just as Laura had feared, her mother was beginning to turn this twinning project into something bigger than Laura wanted it to be.

"I'm only going to visit this lady once," Laura had insisted after she had explained everything to her parents and showed them the information from Rabbi Gardiner. "Maybe she'll have a story about a child from the Holocaust that she can tell me. Then I can combine it with some stuff from my last year's project." And that would be that — simple and straightforward. But Laura's mom had other ideas.

"It would be fascinating if we could do some research on my family tree," her mother had said enthusiastically. "I have distant relatives in Austria and the Czech Republic — cousins of your late grandmother. They and their parents were survivors of the Holocaust. I realize now that we haven't talked enough about that time with you," she added more softly, glancing in the mirror to check on Laura's sister who sat quietly in the back of the car. "No one from our immediate family was involved. Your grandparents were born here and never went through the war in Europe. But I realize that this history is so important to all of us. I haven't been in touch with those relatives in years, but maybe if you wrote to them and explained what you were doing; you could write something about them along with this new story . . ."

"Mom, stop!" Laura had insisted. "My Bat Mitzvah is only a few weeks away. And this is just one visit!"

"I'll be back in an hour." Laura's mother was talking again as she pulled into the driveway of a small low-rise apartment building. "I'm going to take Emma to the mall and get her some new shoes."

Laura's little sister squealed from the back seat of the van. "I want running shoes with lights on them." She had a mop of dark curly hair that bounced up and down each time the car hit a bump in the road.

Laura smiled. "Pink ones, Em?"

Emma nodded enthusiastically. "Pink and yellow. And ice cream after."

"Only if you're good, Emma. That's our deal," Laura's mother said wearily. "Is this the right place?"

Laura glanced down at the sheet of paper. "Yup," she said. "Number 250 Morton Street, apartment 301." It was a modest apartment building in a quiet part of the city.

"Should I come up with you to make sure?" her mother asked.

Laura shook her head. "It's the right place. I'll call you if there's a problem." Laura hated it when her mother became so overprotective, treating her as if she were a child, like Emma.

"Just remember to be polite," her mother said. "And patient, even if you don't understand everything she is saying at first."

"I know, I know." Laura wished her mother would park the car, stop talking, and let her get on with this.

"And remember to thank her at the end for taking the time to talk to you."

"Good-bye, Mom. Have fun, Emma." Laura grabbed her backpack and got out of the car. She waited until her mother had pulled out of the driveway before approaching the door of the building. Laura glanced at the names on the board before pressing the buzzer beside apartment 301. A few seconds passed and then a small voice crackled out of the intercom. "Yes?"

"Uh . . . hello? Mrs. Mandelcorn? I'm Laura Wyman. I called you yesterday." Another few seconds and then the buzzer sounded.

The door to Mrs. Mandelcorn's apartment was open when Laura got off the elevator on the third floor. No one was there. Laura paused and then knocked on the open door. "Hello? Mrs. Mandelcorn? Um . . . it's Laura." What now, she wondered, cautiously poking her head into the empty apartment and glancing around.

"Yes, hello," a voice called out from another room. "Please come in. I'm afraid I'm not quite ready yet. Make yourself comfortable. I'll join you in a moment."

Why are people always late? Laura wondered as she sighed, stepped over the threshold, and gazed around. The apartment was densely furnished with sofas, chairs, and a carved oak dining room table and sideboard. But besides the assortment of furniture, the apartment was filled with wooden sculptures, a collection of vases and

21

flowerpots, porcelain statues, and figurines of all shapes and sizes. It was like walking into one of those antique stores her mother loved so much — overflowing with odds and ends. Two enormous bookshelves dominated one corner of the living room. They sagged under the weight of dozens of books — hard and soft cover, leaning and top-pling onto one another like passengers in a crowded subway. An old upright piano sat in another corner, adorned with family photographs in silver, gold, and wooden frames. Similar photographs covered the walls of the apartment, along with paintings and pencil sketches. Laura paused in front of a particularly beautiful one of a sunset by a lake. It dominated one wall.

"I'm afraid I am a collector of *tchotchkes*." Laura spun around to face the small elderly woman who had entered the room. "I'm so sorry to be late — a bad habit, I'm afraid. I'm so happy to meet you, Laura." Mrs. Mandelcorn was dressed in a stylish pair of black pants and a red sweater. Her shortly cropped hair was neatly brushed behind her ears. From the voice on the telephone, Laura had pictured a weak and frail old woman. But Mrs. Mandelcorn appeared strong and vigorous, even if she was short. She had a warm smile that moved all the way up her face to her twinkling eyes. "Do you know this word, *tchotchkes*?" she asked, sweeping her arm around the room.

Laura shook her head. It sounded as if Mrs. Mandelcorn had said *"theese vord."* Laura was going to have to pay close attention to understand what this woman was saying. Mrs. Mandelcorn laughed softly and her dark eyes crinkled into soft folds. "Ornaments. Little play things. I didn't have many things as a child, and I've more than made up for it now."

Laura glanced back at the photographs on the wall. "My children," said Mrs. Mandelcorn as if reading her mind. "My son and my daughter are both married, and I have five grandchildren," she said proudly. "They don't visit me often enough, but I'm not complaining," she added hastily. "I'm blessed to have them. Come sit down, Laura." When Mrs. Mandelcorn said her name she rolled the 'r', prolonging the sound like a soft musical note — *Laurrrrra*. It was lyrical and sweet.

Mrs. Mandelcorn pushed aside a knitted shawl that had been casually thrown over the sofa and invited Laura to sit down. "I've made you some chocolate cake. Every young person likes chocolate, right?"

Laura nodded and smiled, and accepted a slice of cake and a glass of lemonade.

"I love to bake, but I don't have the opportunity to do much these days. How much cake can an old woman like me eat?"

Laura glanced around. "Do you live by yourself?"

Mrs. Mandelcorn shook her head. "My husband, Max, died many years ago. That's when my younger sister came to live with me. She's not here right now," she added.

"I have a younger sister, too," said Laura, struggling to make conversation. "She's only five."

Mrs. Mandelcorn smiled. "My sister is my best friend. I can't imagine my life without her."

Laura frowned. There were days when she wished she were an only child and Emma wasn't anywhere in her life. Her little sister was cute when she was on her best behavior, but at other times she was whiny and demanding. She had one of those beautiful porcelain faces that everyone loved. And she used her adorable charm to her advantage whenever she could. It infuriated Laura when her parents gave in to Em. "You have lots of books," Laura said, trying to make small talk. "You must love to read."

Mrs. Mandelcorn's eyes lit up. "There are not enough hours in the day to read everything I would like. I was a teacher once, you know? I learned English as a child — mostly from books — and taught it to adults like me who had come from Europe after the war. Can you imagine me, with my accent, teaching English?" Mrs. Mandelcorn laughed again. Laura was beginning to warm up to her.

"Were you in the war too?" Laura regretted the question as soon as the words were out of her mouth. Mrs. Mandelcorn fell silent and a small shadow passed across her eyes. Her shoulders slumped and she turned her face away, gazing for a moment into space. Clearly this was a sensitive topic.

"Well," said Laura, struggling to break the silence. "As I explained on the telephone, Rabbi Gardiner gave me your number and said you might have some information for me. You see, I'm supposed to do this project . . ."

Mrs. Mandelcorn raised her hand. "Yes, Laura. I know why you are here and I have something for you." Without another word, Mrs. Mandelcorn stood up and left the room. Laura wished she could leave as well. This woman was sweet and very kind. But there was sadness in her. She reminded Laura of her mother's Aunt Yvonne, whom her mother had mentioned in the car. Aunt Yvonne had never been the same after her husband died. She cried whenever someone mentioned his name. Mrs. Mandelcorn seemed like that. She tried to cover her sadness with her smile, but Laura could feel that ever-present sorrow and it was intense.

A moment later, Mrs. Mandelcorn returned. "I think everything you want to know is here." With that, she held out a small book. Laura reached out to touch it and then quickly withdrew her hand. There was something here that made her uneasy — she didn't know what.

"Don't be afraid," said Mrs. Mandelcorn, noting Laura's hesitation and pushing the book toward her. "Take it."

Laura took the book and turned it over in her hands, holding it as if it were a fragile piece of glass. It was bound in a deep brown soft leather cover that was shiny in some places, and worn down and rough in others, as if someone had held it in exactly the same way for years. Laura unwound the string that encircled the book, opened it to the first page, and gazed at the youthful handwriting. It was written in a foreign language, but underneath the title page was printed in English, *"The Diary of Sara Gittler, Warsaw Ghetto, 1941-1943."*

"Whose is it?" asked Laura.

"It belonged to a young girl," Mrs. Mandelcorn replied. "It was written in Polish, but I translated it into English a long time ago. The English I learned as a child came in handy, no?"

Another mystery, thought Laura. "I don't quite understa . . . "

"Take it home with you," interrupted Mrs. Mandelcorn. "The rabbi told me you were looking for a story — a child from the Holocaust to remember. Perhaps you will find something here that will help you." Shortly after, Laura said good-bye and left the apartment.

Her mother was waiting outside when Laura emerged. Had a full hour really gone by? It had felt like minutes. Laura was quiet on the ride home. Her mother tried to ask some questions, but Laura wouldn't respond. In the end, Emma made up for both of them; she chatted happily about her new running shoes all the way home. For once, Laura was grateful to have her little sister as a diversion.

Once at home, Laura disappeared quickly into her bedroom, closing the door behind her and sinking onto her bed. In the background, Laura could hear Emma making a fuss about going to bed. Her mom was talking to her, probably trying to make some kind of deal — two stories, three hugs, a glass of water, and then lights out. But Emma would have none of it and continued to wail until her mom's voice rose sharply. Laura's phone rang — probably Nix or Adam calling to ask about her visit to Mrs. Mandelcorn. But Laura ignored the ring. She tried to block out all the sounds and distractions in her home. She stared down at the leather book.

What was her hesitation in opening it? It was the same feeling of uncertainty she had had when Rabbi Gardiner had first talked about the twinning project and when Adam had talked about his grandfather. And Laura was beginning to realize that it wasn't just about feeling stressed and being overworked. The truth was, she always had lots of activities, thrived on them. That wasn't it. The thing that was preventing her from diving into this project was here, between the pages of this book — a fear growing in the pit of Laura's stomach that she was going to find something inside that might be more than she could bear. Was she really ready to jump into this when it felt as if she were leaping from some high place without a net?

Laura shuddered. She had to shake this feeling. If Adam were here, he'd tell her to snap out of it and stop being so melodramatic. He'd quote some Beatles lyrics, something like "take a sad song, and make it better," or something like that. Adam always said that Laura worried about stuff way too much, while he could sum up life in three words — "no big deal." At that thought, Laura smiled and finally opened the leather book. She thumbed through the pages, stopping periodically to stare at the script. The girl who had written this had perfect handwriting; the letters were evenly formed and painstakingly executed. There was hardly one scratched out word. Dates were written at the top of several pages, and in the margins there were hand-drawn simple pictures; a small cat, what looked like a loaf of bread, and an armband with the Star of David, the symbol of the Jewish religion. Finally, Laura turned to the back of the diary and to the typewritten pages that Mrs. Mandelcorn had added. Taking a deep breath, Laura began to read.

July 16, 1941

I love to write. I think I have been writing my whole life — stories, poetry, songs. Whenever I've been excited by a birthday party or a sunset, I've tried to write down how I feel about it. Whenever I have been angry with my parents or teachers, I've turned to writing as a way of expressing those thoughts that are too difficult to say out loud. But here's the thing — my life has become so awful in the past few months that I haven't felt like writing at all. I've avoided my diary. But the truth is I could never stop writing forever. And if there were ever a time when I needed to write things down, now is that time.

We've been here in the ghetto for six months now, but it feels more like six years, six decades, forever! When the walls were finished and everyone was moved inside, we were lucky to find a small apartment for the six of us. Some families have to share with strangers. That's what happened to my friend, Deena, and her parents. They are living with an old couple and Deena says the old man snores and barely even speaks to her. Deena says they are all jammed together the way her grandmother used to bottle pickles — one next to the other until there was no space left in the jar.

At least we've been able to stay together. And by we, I mean my parents, my brother, David, my little sister, Hinda, and my grandmother, Bubbeh. There are six of us crammed into two small rooms here at Wolynska Street number 28, close to Zamenhofa Street. I share a room with Bubbeh. Hinda stays with Mama and Tateh because she's the youngest. David sleeps in the tiny kitchen. He has a cot by the stove.

But many nights he isn't there at all. He goes out and no one knows where he goes.

David is sixteen years old. He has sunny blond hair and blue eyes just like Mama's. But his face is full of clouds. That's what Tateh says when I ask him why David has stopped speaking to me. Tateh says, "David's disposition is like a cloudy day with rainstorms on the horizon." He says David's anger will pass and "his sunny temperament will reappear." Mama says it's just a stage he's going through, that most sixteen-year-old boys go through a time when they become silent and distant. But David has been angry for years, ever since things became worse for Jews in Warsaw. The worst day for David was the day he was no longer allowed to go to school. That was at about the same time as when they changed the name of Pilsudski Square in downtown Warsaw to Adolf Hitler Square, and declared it off limits to Jews. I don't think David's anger is going to let up soon at all.

Hinda is only six. I don't think she can really remember a time in her life that was different from the way things are now. She has always lived with rules about what she can and mostly can't do. She has only known a life where she must be afraid of being Jewish. Hinda has an imaginary friend whose name is Julia. Julia takes Hinda to the zoo and to the park, and places we all used to go to before they were forbidden to Jews.

And then there's me. I'm right in the middle — twelve years old. I'm short — too short if you ask me — and I have brown eyes and dark wavy hair. I know I look like my Tateh and I don't mean to complain, but

I wish I didn't. Don't get me wrong, I adore my father. He is gentle and loving and strong. But I do wish I looked more like Mama. Everyone says she is pretty. She has soft delicate features. Even though her hair is dull these days and she has lost so much weight, I still see how beautiful she is.

No one says that about me. They say I'm smart, and I am. I used to stand first in my class, when I was still allowed to go to school. Tateh tells me I'm beautiful all the time, but that's just because he's my Tateh. My features are sharp. My mouth is wide and I have annoying freckles across my nose and cheeks that are even more noticeable when I am in the sun. Just once, I wish someone besides Tateh would tell me I was beautiful.

Adolf Hitler had dark hair and eyes.

It's funny. When Hitler was deciding who would be part of his perfect race, he decided that it would only include people who were Aryan — those with blue eyes and blond hair, which is how many Germans look. If you had dark features like me and Tateh and so many Jews, you couldn't be part of Hitler's perfect race, and you were targeted for discrimination. But here's the thing. Mama and David are blond and delicate, while Hitler has dark eyes and a large nose. I've never seen him in real life but I've seen his picture on posters. So, in that perfect world that Hitler has imagined, Mama and David should be included while Hitler himself should be left out! I know it's not that simple. I know it's not just about how we look. I know it's about who we are — Jews. And Jews don't belong in Hitler's perfect world. But it is ironic, don't you think?

So that's us — David, Hinda, and me. We are so different — in age, in how we act, and how we look. But in the end, there is something the same about the three of us and that is that we are all trying to escape this prison in some way. David escapes the hard times by becoming silent. Hinda escapes by using her imagination. I write my thoughts down. I guess we all need our own escape.

Sara Gittler

August 12, 1941

Deena Katz is my best friend. We've known each other forever, even before the ghetto. We grew up in houses next to each other and we used to be in the same class at school. Thank goodness she's here in the ghetto. I can't imagine being here without a friend.

We look nothing alike, Deena and me. Just like my brother, David, Deena is tall and blond. But my Tateh says we could be sisters — twins even. We finish each other's sentences as if we knew what the other one was thinking. Deena is an only child, so she loves telling everyone that I'm her sister. People stare at us, wondering how two such different looking girls could be related. And then Deena just laughs and walks away.

Deena is one of the most talented people I know. She can draw better than anyone. She wants to be a famous artist one day and I bet she will become one. She can draw anything and make it look better than the real thing. Not like me; I draw sticks with circles on top, and I call those my people.

When we first moved to the ghetto, Deena told me that she brought her sketch paper and colored pencils. It seems like each of us brought something special and personal into the ghetto — something to remember the life we once knew. I brought a few of my favorite books, like *War with the Newts*, written by Karel Capek, who is a very famous author from Czechoslovakia. The story is about a group of giant lizards that grow stronger and stronger until they are at war with mankind. I think I've read that book so many times I could almost recite it from heart. I've even learned to speak a little English after using a dictionary to work my way through *How Green Was My Valley* by Richard Llewellyn. My cousin, Dvora, who lives in England, once sent it to me for my birthday. I love the sound of English words. That book is about a family living in Wales, the Morgans. There are seven children in the family; the youngest is ten-year-old Huw Morgan who tells the story. The family is poor and they struggle every day just to get by. But they love one another, and that's what keeps them going despite their hardships. I can relate to both of those books and the stories they tell. The lizards are evil monsters, just like the Nazis, getting stronger and more dangerous each day. And my family is close and loving like the Morgans. Despite everything that has happened to us, we depend on each other now more than ever. I think that's why I love those books so much. They are so close to the life I am living.

Tateh brings home books from time to time. He gets them on the black market, trading for them with a piece of Mama's china or an old record. Mama always looks annoyed. She says, "Books won't fill our

People bartered for books and other things in the ghetto.

empty stomachs." She wants Tateh to barter for flour, or vegetables, or even a warm scarf for the coming winter.

But Tateh always replies, "Books nourish the soul. And that, too, is important. I'll go without the scarf to see my Sara read," he adds as Mama makes that "tsk, tsk" sound and turns away.

But back to Deena. I know she is running low on sketch paper and her colored pencils are becoming smaller. "I can only draw the most important things now," she says. "I can't waste any paper." Deena stares at me from behind her glasses. She has to be so careful with them — they are the only pair she owns. And if they get broken, then Deena says it doesn't matter how many colored pencils she has. She won't be able to see or draw a thing!

If you ask me, none of Deena's pictures are a waste. Each one is beautiful. Deena has given me a few of her sketches — the ones I love most. There's the one of the robin that she sketched when it landed miraculously in the courtyard a few weeks ago. I hadn't seen a bird in so long and I almost cried out loud. But Deena shushed me, pulled out her sketch pad, and quickly drew the robin while it posed for her. But my favorite drawing of all is the one of the sun setting on a blue lake. It reminds me of the northern part of Poland by the Baltic Sea where we used to go for family holidays in the summer. I've told Deena that I'll keep her drawings forever and when she's famous, we'll put them in an exhibition that everyone will come and see.

Sometimes Deena feels as if she has to hurry to draw. She says, "I have to create as many pictures as I possibly can before . . ."

"Don't say it!" I shout angrily at her, knowing even before the words are out of her mouth that she is going to say that things in the ghetto are only getting worse. I don't want to think of anything bad that might happen and I don't want Deena to talk of these things. But deep down, I understand what Deena is trying to say, that there won't be time to do the things she needs to do. Something is going to happen and we are all waiting for it. Even though we are locked inside these ghetto walls, we can't forget the world that is outside. But the bits of news that reach us from beyond the gates of the ghetto are never good.

David tells me that there are ghettos just like this one in Kovno, Minsk, Bialystok, and Lvov. We have relatives in all of those cities, and I wonder if they, like us, are living behind walls and gates with nothing to eat and nowhere to go. It sounds like the Nazi armies are getting stronger and more powerful. They have invaded other countries like Yugoslavia and the Soviet Union. They have arrested Jews in Paris and other cities. We hear that information from people on the street. They spread the news to one another in whispers. I know there are radios in the ghetto even though it's forbidden to own one. And sometimes, even though it scares me to hear the news, I am forcing myself to listen. I have to know what's happening. Maybe if I know, I'll be able to do something — help in some way. Tateh says that things will get better soon, but I don't think he is telling the truth. And if he isn't telling the truth about that, then what else is he keeping from me?

Sara Gittler

Chapter Four

Laura had barely begun to read the diary when she was interrupted by her mother knocking gently on her bedroom door and then entering without waiting for a response. She was not pleased to see Laura still awake. "Honey, you've got to turn out the lights and get some sleep," her mother said.

"I will, Mom," Laura replied, quickly pushing the journal under her blanket. She wasn't yet ready to talk to her mother about what she was reading. "I've still got some work to finish."

Her mother hesitated. "You've had too many late nights, Laura," she finally said firmly. "You need to sleep. Now!"

Reluctantly, Laura rolled over and switched off the light. But she was still awake long after her mother left the room. Something about the diary was tugging at her, though she wasn't sure what it was. She was still nervous about what she was going to discover written there, and she didn't know how to deal with that. She certainly wasn't ready to commit to the twinning project. And yet, just as the girl in the journal needed to know more about the facts of the war, Laura needed to know more about that girl — about Sara. It was a bit like watching one of those horror movies that Nix always brought over, the kind that you watched with one eye open, wanting to know what was going to happen, but terrified that there would be gory parts.

"I was trying to call you last night," said Adam the next day as he and Laura left their last class together. Laura had raced from class to class all day. This was the first opportunity she had to talk to Adam. "So? Where were you?" he asked.

Laura shrugged. "I was reading."

"Only you can get so lost in a book that you don't even answer the phone," groaned Adam, shaking his head and staring at his friend. "So, what was it this time? Fantasy? Mystery? Biography?"

"Kind of a bit of everything, I guess," Laura replied and went on to tell Adam about her visit to Mrs. Mandelcorn and the journal she had received. "I don't know where it came from, or how this old lady got it," she explained. "The girl who wrote it talks about what it was like to be discriminated against just because she was Jewish."

Adam nodded. "Like my grandfather. I told you his stories were amazing."

Laura frowned. "I guess." She couldn't admit that she was curious about the journal and drawn to the stories, even thought she hadn't stopped thinking about them all day.

"So what are you going to do with it?" asked Adam. The two walked slowly down a set of stairs, dodging the throng of students who were rushing to get out of the building at the end of the day. Adam had his backpack slung over his shoulder. He carried one large textbook in his arms, cradling it as if it were a guitar, and pretending to strum the back cover.

"I'm supposed to figure out a way to use it in my Bat Mitzvah," explained Laura, shaking her head. "But I don't know how. I haven't read that much," she added. But from the short amount she had read, Laura was already recognizing that the girl who had written the stories — Sara — wasn't all that different from herself; they were the same age, had siblings, close friends, and enjoyed some of the same things. The exception to this was that Laura and Sara were living in radically different circumstances. Laura could come and go as she pleased, when she pleased, but Sara was cooped up as if she was in a prison, a prison that was harsh and cruel.

"You'll figure it out," said Adam, thoughtfully. "Look," he added. "When the Beatles first got together they didn't know they would change everything about music forever."

Laura shook her head. "Adam, I'm not trying to change history. I'm just trying to get through the next few weeks." Adam's obsession with the Beatles could go too far sometimes.

"You never know what'll happen." Adam struck a pose with his textbook, swinging it up into the air as he started to sing the chorus to "Let it Be."

Ignoring him, Laura strained her neck trying to see if Nix was anywhere in sight. They were supposed to meet after school and ride their bikes home together, but Laura never knew if Nix would keep her waiting long after the bell had sounded and the school had cleared out for the day. No matter how hard she tried, Laura had never been able to cure Nix of lateness. "I've tried to be on time," Nix often said. "But it's kind of like buying ice cream. When I walk in the store I'm determined to try a new flavor, but I always go back to vanilla chocolate chip. You're never going to change me." Miraculously, Laura spotted her friend, chatting with some other students at the front door. She reached up to wave, but Nix didn't see her.

Adam was still strumming his textbook and singing at the top of his lungs. *There will be an answer, let it be.* His eyes were partly closed as he moved down the stairs. Laura was just going to warn him to watch where he was going when suddenly Adam tripped beside her, losing his footing, and stumbling on the steps. His textbook left his arms, sailing into the air and down the length of the staircase, landing with a thud against the back of an older boy who was standing at the bottom.

"What the . . ." The boy turned slowly and stared up at Adam. He reached up to rub the back of his neck and then looked around, bending to retrieve the textbook before slowly climbing the stairs, two of his friends close behind him.

Adam froze and Laura felt her heart begin to race. It was Steve Collins, a ninth grader. He was tall and broadly built. As usual, his sidekicks were behind him. They were shorter than Steve, but also older students. The three of them had a reputation for being tough and mean.

"This yours?" asked Steve as he stopped inches from Adam's face and held out the textbook. He had long stringy hair parted in the middle and wore a black T-shirt and torn blue jeans.

"I'm . . . yeah . . . I'm . . ." Adam stuttered and stumbled over his words, then took a deep breath and started again. "I'm really sorry. I wasn't looking."

"Wasn't looking?" Steve moved even closer to Adam. "You think that's an excuse for pounding me with your book?"

"It was an accident. I . . . I promise." Adam nervously adjusted his glasses. His hands were trembling.

"No such thing as accidents," said Steve as his two friends stepped up behind him.

This wasn't good, thought Laura. Adam had done nothing deliberate, but she knew that boys like Steve Collins didn't need an excuse to bully. She looked around, desperate for help. Most of the students had left for the day. Those few remaining had stopped, watching and waiting to see what would happen. Laura caught Nix's eye at the bottom of the staircase, but she, too, was frozen. Adam was white as a ghost. He seemed to shrink under the glare of the three older boys.

"Is there a problem here, Mr. Collins?" The school principal, Mr.

Garrett, was walking up the stairs toward the boys. Someone must have gone to get him, and not a moment too soon.

As soon as he heard Mr. Garrett's voice, Steve relaxed his body, stepped away from Adam, and turned to greet the principal. "No problem, Mr. G.," he said, smiling broadly. "This kid dropped a book and I was just returning it." He tossed the textbook over to Adam who was barely able to catch it. Adam was visibly shaken and still pale.

Mr. Garrett looked closely at Steve and his friends, and then glanced over at Adam. "Are you all right, Mr. Segal?"

Adam nodded weakly. "I'm fine," he said.

Mr. Garrett paused, sizing up the situation. Finally he nodded. "Then I would suggest you move on, Mr. Collins, and let everyone get home."

Steve grinned at the principal. Before leaving, he turned his head to glare at Adam, and whispered over his shoulder so that only Adam and Laura could hear what he was saying. "Loser," he sneered. "Watch it!" Then he grinned broadly once more and sauntered off, his two buddies close behind him.

"Are you sure you're okay?" asked Mr. Garrett after the older boys had left.

Adam shrugged his shoulders. "It's no big deal," he said. Laura wasn't fooled. Adam was badly shaken and she could see it.

Mr. Garrett paused a moment more. Then he nodded and moved off.

For a moment, neither Laura nor Adam moved. Laura's mind

raced over the incident and what might have been if Mr. Garrett hadn't come along. Finally, she turned to face Adam. "I thought for sure he was going to punch you or something," she said, reaching out to grab Adam's arm.

Adam was sweating and breathing heavily, as if he had just finished a race. "Yeah, that was close."

"Adam, why didn't you say something to him?" Nix had raced up the stairs to join her friends.

"Like what?" asked Adam.

"Like telling him to back off. You can't let people like him bully you," Nix replied.

Adam shrugged. "Nah. Better to ignore them. No big deal," he added again. "Did you hear what he said to me?" he asked and then repeated Steve's last threat.

"That guy acts all tough. He says stuff like that to everyone who gets in his way. Don't worry about it too much," said Nix.

Adam, Nix, and Laura walked down the stairs and out of the school building. The cool afternoon breeze was just what Laura needed. She had felt as if she were suffocating inside the school. But here, in the fresh air, she caught her breath and tried to relax. Despite what Nix had said, it was all still scary to her. She knew these boys had a reputation for bullying students in the school, often picking on smaller weaker students who wouldn't stand up for themselves. But this was the first time she had been close to someone who was being threatened. Laura looked over at Adam. He still looked pale.

Laura's mind continued to race. One minute everything had been so normal, so predictable. She had been laughing and talking with Adam with no worries about her friend's safety or her own. The next minute Adam was being threatened and she felt helpless to do anything about it. Laura wished she could take the incident, crumple it into a tight ball, and throw it into a garbage can. If only it were that simple.

"I'm just going to ride on my own for a while," Laura said as she and her friends reached the bike stands. They had said little since leaving the school. "I'll call you later," she added, pulling her helmet from her backpack and looking at Adam.

"Remember we're going shopping tomorrow afternoon," said Nix.

Laura waved over her shoulder, but didn't answer. Shopping was the last thing on her mind. She needed to get home. She needed to be by herself where she could think more clearly about what had happened and what it all meant. Perhaps there were more similarities between her life and Sara's life than she had at first realized. It scared Laura to think that. But it also made her desperate to know more about Sara. Laura needed to close the door to her bedroom and continue to read.

August 27, 1941

The ghetto walls that surround our apartment and the other buildings are scary. They were built by Jewish men including Tateh and David. My Tateh once had the softest hands, but I watched as they became rough and sore and would bleed all the time. Tateh never complained about the work. But late at night, when he thought I wasn't watching, I could see Mama tending to the cuts and blisters. Only then would I catch him cringe and pull away, and I imagined how hard the work must be.

Jewish men built the ghetto walls.

Tateh is a teacher. He taught in the same elementary school that I used to attend — that is, until he lost his job, and I lost my right to go to school. I never had him as a teacher, but his students were always coming up to me and telling me that he was the best teacher they had ever had. Tateh loved to teach; he loved inspiring others to learn.

Now Tateh works in a German shoe factory. Each day, he and a group of men are marched out the gates of the ghetto to the factory where he sits at a machine all day long. He cuts and sands wooden shoes and boots that are being made for German soldiers. I've watched his hands become harder and rougher until they look almost like the leather in the shoes that he is making. He's lucky to have the job, he says. He gets a few extra rations of food for the rest of us. Since we've been here, the word, "lucky" has come to mean something completely different from what it once was. Lucky used to mean finding a zloty coin on the road and using it to buy a candy. Now, lucky means knowing your father has a backbreaking, boring job. Lucky means having a few extra pieces of bread for your family.

When Tateh was a teacher, books were the only things he used to lift. But to build the walls of the ghetto, he and the other Jewish men had to drag loads of bricks and enormous stones to pile one on top of the other. They slathered mud and clay in between the stones. And on the top layer, the men placed pieces of broken glass, jutting upward into the sky like sharp blades. As if that weren't threatening enough, they strung lines of barbed wire across the top to complete the wall.

Once it was finished, we moved in, passing through the gate that was to enclose us inside this prison. "We're building our own jail," David would say angrily, and Tateh would shake his head and sigh.

"We're lucky that we are together inside. That's what is most important," he would say. There was that word again, "lucky." I don't feel lucky, and I'm not sure what is worse, living outside the walls where Jews are hated and mistreated, or living inside where we are forgotten.

Sara Gittler

August 28, 1941

I have a terrible cold and feel miserable. Mama has no medicine to give me to help me feel better. There aren't even any tissues for my runny nose. I hope no one else gets sick.

Sara Gittler

September 6, 1941

We had a piano in our real home and Mama used to give lessons to the neighborhood children after school. And on top of the piano there was an old metronome. Mama said it came from Zamek Krelewski, the man who taught her to play when she was a child. She would set it and turn it on to help her students keep the beat of the piece they were learning. I could always tell who had practiced that week from the sound of the piano working alongside the metronome. Hirsch Rublach was Mama's worst student. He never practiced at all. I don't even know why he bothered with the lessons except that his mother wanted him to learn to play, and I guess he couldn't say no to her.

When Mama turned on the metronome and Hirsch played, it was like winding up the old gramophone and listening to the tune pick up speed. Tock, tock, tock — the metronome kept perfect time, but Hirsch was a mess. He started slow, beats behind the metronome, then picked up speed until he sailed past the ticking sound into a piano frenzy, then slow again. Fast and slow, back and forth — so many times it made me dizzy and I had to shove my fists into my mouth to keep from laughing out loud.

I don't know what has become of Hirsch or so many of Mama's students. I wonder if they managed to somehow get out of Poland before the war closed in on all of us. I wonder if they are alive. The metronome is gone — so is the piano — left behind in the move to the ghetto. When the Nazi soldiers march outside my window during the day, their boots make the same clicking sound as that metronome, only louder. No one is out of step. No one marches too fast or too slow. The Nazis keep perfect time.

Sara Gittler

September 18, 1941

When we first went into the ghetto, I couldn't bring my cat, and that was probably the worst moment in my life. I had had my cat for two years. I found him when he was just a kitten, crying in an alley close to my home. I scooped him up and took him home, knowing Mama would fall in love with him at first glance. And I was right. We named him Feliks which means "lucky," because I thought he was lucky that I had come along to rescue him. Feliks was sweet and cuddly, followed me everywhere, and slept on a blanket at the foot of my bed — even though Mama disapproved.

But when I was putting aside Feliks's blanket to take into the ghetto, I could feel Mama's eyes on me. At first I tried to ignore her. But finally, she took me by the shoulders and turned me around. "Listen, my darling," Mama said, as I tried to pull away and cover my ears. "We will barely have enough space for ourselves in the ghetto, or enough money for our own food. We can't possibly take Feliks." I sobbed, not wanting to believe I would have to leave Feliks behind. But I knew I had no choice.

Before leaving our home, I took Feliks to our neighbor next door. Mrs. Kaminski is a Catholic woman. She hadn't had much to do with my family for many months. I don't think she liked us very much because we were Jewish. Or maybe she was just afraid of what would happen to her if she was friendly or helpful to a Jewish family. But I knew she loved cats, and she agreed to take Feliks. Deena came with me that day. She knew how hard it would be for me to say good-bye to my beautiful Feliks.

Mrs. Kaminski barely looked at me when I knocked on her door. She just held out her arms. I handed over Feliks's soft pillow, his blanket, playing toys, and the last bag of food we had. Then I handed over Feliks, not before giving him one last hug and kiss, burying my nose in his soft downy fur.

Thanking Mrs. Kaminski, I turned to go. I did not want her to see me cry. "Feliks will be fine," Deena said, but she looked sad, too. As I climbed the stairs to my apartment, I could not help but think that I was doing something that was wrong. I felt as if I was abandoning my beautiful pet. Here we were as Jews, being abandoned and forced to leave our homes. And I was doing the same thing to Feliks! And even though we were human beings and Feliks was an animal, I was so sad to see him left behind. I tried to shake these thoughts away.

"I know you're right, Deena," I finally said. "Mrs. Kaminski will take care of Feliks." But at the same time, I wondered if we would manage as well.

Besides the agonizing decision over Feliks, it was impossible to decide what to take when we went to live in the ghetto, but even more difficult to decide what to leave behind. I didn't want to leave anything. Can you imagine having to choose between your favorite records or books or toys — the one or two most special things that you will take with you? Impossible! But that's what we had to do.

"We won't have much space in our apartment, and the little space we do have will be taken up with clothes, blankets, and essential things," said Mama.

So I sorted through my belongings. I knew that for every one thing I would bring with me into the ghetto, I would have to leave ten things behind.

As hard as it was for me, it was nearly impossible for Hinda. Try explaining to a six-year-old that most of her toys will be left behind.

She couldn't understand it at all. She sobbed and sobbed about having to leave her favorite dolls, and she finally fell asleep in Mama's arms, exhausted from all her crying.

Tateh had the same difficulty sorting through his record collection. "How does one choose between Tchaikovsky and Mozart?" he muttered. In the end, it didn't matter. We didn't bring the gramophone with us into the ghetto to play the records. Music, it turned out, was less important than food and clothing.

Sara Gittler

October 1, 1941

Tateh started singing last night. It was cold in our ghetto apartment and we were all at the small table in the kitchen, trying to capture the last bit of warmth from the stove. Even David was there. At first, no one was talking. It was as if each one of us was somewhere else, off daydreaming, perhaps thinking of a lovely memory from the past, or wishing we were anywhere but here. Then Hinda started talking to her imaginary friend. "Would you like some biscuits, Julia?" Hinda asked, pretending to hold a plate in her hands. "Only one biscuit for now. We'll save the rest for later."

David wanted Hinda to stop and snapped something at her, but Mama hushed him, reminding him that Hinda is still a child and needs her fantasies. David finally put his head down on the table and didn't move.

I barely noticed any of this. I was thinking about the party that Deena had had for her twelfth birthday. Boys and girls were there and Avrom Zusman even asked me to dance. Of course I blushed so deeply that Deena said I looked like a tomato. That made me blush even more!

So, there we were at the small table when suddenly Tateh started to sing an old Yiddish folk song. *"Wus geven is geven un nitu,"* he sang.

I only have memories of days gone by,
The year has left, the hours slip away.
How quickly my joy disappears
And it can't be captured back, not ever, not today.

What once was no longer is,
The strong grow weak, all those we knew.
But I believe in myself and what once was,
We know we will cope, we will make do.

Tateh has a beautiful deep voice that echoes with each note. At first, we were all so startled; no one said anything. Hinda stopped talking to Julia and David lifted his head. We listened to Tateh sing with our own mouths wide open. But then, Mama began to hum along, then Bubbeh, and pretty soon all of us were singing and harmonizing with Tateh's melody. It was a sad song, but it reminded me of home. And for a brief moment, the ghetto walls faded away and I felt peaceful — maybe even lucky!

Sara Gittler

October 27, 1941

It was pouring with rain when I woke up this morning and even though I didn't go outside, I could feel the cold and dampness inside our apartment. I could see the tiny drops that gathered on the pipe above the stove and could hear as they plopped inside the bucket that Mama had placed in the middle of the floor. Before we moved to the ghetto, I used to love the rain, used to love standing outside underneath a rain shower with my head back and my mouth wide open, trying to catch drops on my tongue. But here, the rainstorms find their way through my thin jacket and under my skin.

I was standing by the window, watching the rain pound on the pavement below. The ghetto streets are filled with ruts and trenches that turn into fast-flowing rivers during a rainstorm, making it even harder to walk. That's when Bubbeh walked toward me and called me Saraleh out of the blue. She hadn't called me by that special name in so long, not since we were home — in our real home, before the ghetto, and I was so startled that I turned away from the storm outside and smiled at her.

When we were in our real home, I used to watch my grandmother make babka, the sweet cinnamon cake that I loved so much. First, Bubbeh mixed flour, eggs, butter, yeast, and milk together to make a soft, sticky dough. And when she kneaded it in the bowl, working it into a shiny ball, it made a sucking noise that reminded me of the loud kisses she used to give me when I came home from school. "Oy, Saraleh. I've missed you," she would say, covering me in those kisses. "Come, tell me everything you learned at school today." And I did — sitting on the high stool next to the counter while watching her make babka. Her arms shook like jelly when she pounded the dough on the counter. And then the best part was when she pulled off a small piece of dough for me and let me shape it into whatever I wanted. Sometimes I made a turtle, and sometimes a tree. My small shape always baked faster than Bubbeh's round babka. And when she pulled my shapes out of the oven and gave them to me, they were still hot and steaming. I never felt too grown up to be with Bubbeh, shaping and baking my small cakes.

That was the last time Bubbeh smiled. That was the last time she called me Saraleh and gave me big kisses. Now she sits quietly, and sometimes, when she thinks I'm not looking, she cries and doesn't stop, even when Tateh tries to tell her that everything will be okay. Mama says nothing. She doesn't even try to make Bubbeh feel better. It's as if sadness is just the way things are these days. And Bubbeh isn't the only one who is sad. Just walk on the street for a minute or two and everyone looks sad. Can you imagine that? The whole Warsaw Ghetto is full of unhappy people.

Bubbeh's arms have lost the round fat that made them wobble. Now they are like small skinny twigs. And her face is thin and so pale it has become almost transparent. The lines around her mouth and eyes are deep like the deep ruts in the pavement outside my window. And when Bubbeh cries it is like rivers of rain from outside running through those ruts and furrows.

I never knew my grandparents on my father's side; they died when

I was a baby. But my mother's father, my Zaideh, died just a year before the wall was built. He had a weak heart that just suddenly stopped one night as he slept. And he never woke up. That's when Bubbeh came to live with us.

I miss my Zaideh. He was funny and he used to do silly tricks with me and Hinda, making a zloty coin disappear and then magically pulling it out from behind my ear. I never told him that I actually knew how the trick worked; I had figured it out years earlier. It would have spoiled the pleasure my Zaideh got each time he repeated the trick — which he did just about every time I saw him.

As much as I miss my Zaideh, a part of me is glad that he died before all of this. I'm relieved he's not here to witness this misery, or to watch Bubbeh cry day after day. This would have destroyed him. Instead, at least I have the memory of his smile and his silly lovely tricks. That memory is as sweet as the one of my grandmother baking babka with me.

Sara Gittler

November 5, 1941

Here's the scariest thing. A few days ago, Hinda came down with a high fever and she said her ear hurt. It got worse and worse as the day went on until she was screaming in pain. Mama sat with her in the bedroom, rocking her, bathing her forehead with cool water, and trying to calm her down, while Tateh paced in the kitchen. I had never seen him look this worried and it scared me. I didn't know what to do. I was so afraid that Hinda might die. I was sorry for all the bad things I ever thought about her; how annoyed we all used to get when she talked on and on about Julia. I just wanted Hinda to get well.

Finally, David went over to Tateh and spoke quietly to him. I didn't know what they were saying but Tateh looked angry at first. He shouted, "I won't have you doing something so dangerous. You could be killed. What good will that do any of us?" David kept talking until Tateh finally lowered his head and nodded meekly. It was as if the struggle with David had robbed my father of his strength. When David finally left the apartment Tateh sat with his head in his hands — in that one position, without moving.

Bubbeh was frantic through this whole time. "I hope he brings me medicine so I can end my life. I can't watch my family suffer." We all ignored Bubbeh, even though I felt a bit bad about that. I think we were just so worried about Hinda and David that we had no energy left to worry about Bubbeh.

I tried to talk to Tateh. I tried to find out what was going on — where David had gone, what was going to happen to Hinda. But Tateh wouldn't move. So I went to David's cot and just sat there, watching Tateh and waiting. I wished in that moment that I could be like David, that I could do something, run somewhere, not just sit helplessly and watch things happen.

When David returned about two hours later, he had a small bottle of liquid in his hands. He held it out to Tateh who grabbed it and then grabbed David, hugging him and murmuring something in his ears. Tears were rolling down Tateh's face.

I don't know if David begged for the medicine or stole it or beat someone up for it. All I know is that Hinda's fever went down and her ear was better in two days.

There once was a fire in my school back at home. No one knew how it started but the whole school had to be evacuated quickly. The teachers tried to keep us calm and orderly, but many of my classmates started to panic, especially the little ones. I remember walking in a line of students, all pushing to get out of the small building as fast as we could. I was also scared, not knowing how bad the fire was, terrified that I wouldn't get out in time. It was only when I stood outside and saw the thick smoke billowing out of the school window, that I realized how lucky I was and how close we had all been to being caught in the fire.

That's what Hinda's illness was like for me. It was like running to get out of a burning building before something really terrible happened. We were able to avoid this disaster. But it always feels as if the next one is just around the corner. Next time I'm going to do something. Next time I'm going to be like David.

Sara Gittler

Chapter Five

"You've got to stop thinking about what happened to Adam," said Nix.

Nix and Laura were shopping at the mall, trying to find a dress for Laura's Bat Mitzvah party. Laura already had the outfit she would wear for the synagogue service — a modest dark skirt and soft pink sweater. She had hunted for days with her mother for something that was appropriate for the occasion but also modern and youthful. "Something you'll wear more than this one time," her mother had said. The skirt and sweater they had found were perfect.

But when it came to the party dress, Laura's mother agreed to let Laura and Nix go shopping on their own. "As long as it's in the budget," her mother said as she dropped them at the entrance to the mall. "And remember," she added. "I still get final approval." Laura knew that meant it had to be what her mother always called, "age appropriate."

"Even if your Bat Mitzvah means you're becoming a young woman, remember you're still a young girl in this family."

Nix was giddy in the mall, enthusiastically rummaging through the racks of trendy skirts and dresses in the junior section of the department store. Laura followed, slowly and reluctantly, still preoccupied with the incident at school — and with Sara's diary.

"Adam's fine," said Nix. "Nothing really happened."

Laura frowned. Nix was so easygoing; she took most things in stride. And Laura admired that about her. But was she being too laid back here, ignoring something that was important? "I know Adam's okay," Laura said.

By the time Laura had called Adam on the evening of the incident, he was acting as if it had never taken place. A Beatles CD was blaring in the background. Adam was quoting seemingly meaningless facts.

"Did you know," said Adam, "that when John wrote "I am the Walrus," it was because he was sick of people trying to interpret his lyrics? So he decided to write something meaningless, just to see what they'd say! Isn't that crazy?"

Laura had laughed, relieved to know that Adam was fine. Nix was probably right. Even though the episode with Steve Collins had scared her, nothing *had* happened, and Laura needed to put it out of her mind.

"It's not only that," Laura said to Nix and went on to tell her about the journal she had received from Mrs. Mandelcorn. "The writing is amazing, Nix. And it's all been done by this Jewish girl our age. You won't believe what her life was like during the war. Her whole family — six of them — were all crammed into two small rooms, inside this ghetto."

Nix frowned curiously.

"You know that there were those places called concentration camps — prisons where lots of Jews were sent."

"Like Anne Frank."

"Right," nodded Laura. "Like Anne Frank after the Nazi soldiers raided her hiding place. Well, even before the concentration camps, there were parts of cities and towns in Europe where Jewish families had to go and live. The Nazis built walls around these sections, with barbed wire and everything. Jews couldn't leave. And inside the ghettos, families were starving, and there was no electricity and no toilets . . ."

"Gross," interrupted Nix.

"Anyway, this girl, Sara, wrote about her life in the ghetto, and that's what I was reading." Laura could hardly begin to explain what it was like to read the journal entries from the leather-bound book. "Some of it's written like a diary. But most of it is like reading a novel, except that it's real." The night before, Laura had finished reading the part about Hinda's illness. And again, she had stayed awake for far too long thinking about what that must have been like for Sara's family. What if the same thing happened in Laura's family? What if Emma became so ill and close to death? Laura never really thought about life and death situations — how many kids her age did? She could read about a war in another country and feel sad. She could know about poverty in Africa and try to help in some way, like she did with her project. But to really put herself in the shoes of people who suffered was something completely different. And that's what seemed to be happening as she was reading Sara's journal. Laura felt as if she was moving closer and closer to Sara's life — closer to Sara. This wasn't a novel and it wasn't a history textbook. The words on the page were real; the lives were real.

"Okay, this one, or this one." Nix held two dresses up in front of her. "I kind of like the silver one because it would be great with your dark hair. But the red one is kind of cute as well."

Laura didn't answer. Her mind was somewhere else, thinking about the life of the girl in the diary. *I wonder how much Sara thought about shopping for new clothes? Or was she only worried about food and her family?*

"Hey! Snap out of it!" Nix interrupted Laura's thoughts.

"Huh? What? Oh, sorry. I guess I'm just not in the mood to shop. I can't explain it."

Nix eyed Laura closely. "What's the matter with you?" asked Nix, tossing her blond hair over her shoulder and flashing her cool, blue eyes. "You look like you've just been grounded for not getting an A on your history test or something like that. You've got your mom's credit card in your hand and a building full of clothes. What could be better? I'm trying to help you here, but you've got to work with me."

"I know. You're right." Laura shook her head and focused on the dresses that Nix was holding out in front of her. "I'm thinking something in blue would be better," she finally said. *Blue! Like how I'm feeling*. Those thoughts she kept to herself.

Nix smiled. "That's better," she said. "Let's find the bluest, most beautiful dress ever."

Laura laughed and smiled fondly at her friend. Nix *was* right. There were wonderful things going on in Laura's life. And she wanted to take the time to enjoy them. By the time Laura got home from the mall she was exhausted but happy. She had found the perfect dress. It was deep blue with thin spaghetti straps and a taffeta crinoline underneath the wide skirt that flared whenever Laura twirled. Her mom had nodded approvingly. But as Laura was taking off the dress and hanging it carefully in her closet, her eyes fell upon the journal lying on the small table next to her bed. And once again, she felt her mood shift.

Laura moved toward her bedside table and picked up the diary, turning it over in her hands, and then opening it to the place where she had finished reading the night before. The next entry was brief.

Nov. 7, 1941

Deena used up the last of her drawing paper today. She drew a group
of children standing in the middle of the street. They were begging for
food, but they were smiling at the people rushing past them. Can you
imagine that? Starving children who are smiling! Deena said she wanted
to capture those smiles in her drawing. When she finished, she closed
her sketch pad, removed her glasses, looked at me, and said, "That's it.
I think I've drawn my last picture." Deena stared at me. Her eyes were
blank and dull. "What am I going to do now?" She whispered that part
as if all the joy in her life was gone. I'm afraid that Deena thinks that if
she can't draw, then what else is there to give her life meaning? I didn't
know what to say to her. I'm going to search for paper. I'm going to tear
out the back blank pages of some of my books. I know how important
it is for Deena to draw. That's what makes her smile.

Sara Gittler

Children begged for food in the ghetto.

It broke Laura's heart to read this short passage, to realize that something as small as drawing paper could be so important in the world in which Sara was living. Laura realized that she was beginning to think of Sara as a friend. She even imagined that she looked a bit like Sara; they both had dark hair and eyes. And Laura had the same annoying freckles across her nose that Sara described. Laura's phone rang and she moved to her desk to answer it.

"Wasn't that the best time?" Nix's voice was bubbling over with excitement.

Laura was so preoccupied with the diary that for a moment, she had no idea what Nix was referring to.

"I mean, what could be better than shopping all afternoon? Hey, do you want to come over? I can make popcorn and we can watch TV."

Laura closed her eyes and took a deep breath before answering. "No, I don't think so. I've still got homework to do, and I just want to read a bit more of this diary." Why was there this growing irritation in the pit of Laura's stomach?

There was a long moment of silence on the other end of the phone. When Nix finally spoke, her voice was cool. "I thought you didn't care about this whole twinning thing."

"I didn't. But something has gotten to me since I started to read Sara's journal." Why didn't Nix get that? "Forget it," said Laura. "I've got to go." She hung up the phone and stared down at the diary. Why was it suddenly so difficult to talk to Nix — to explain to her how she was feeling? It was frustrating to discover that Nix couldn't seem to grasp the importance of all of this. Laura didn't want to start a fight but it was beginning to feel as if she and Nix were talking two different languages. It was always the differences between herself and Nix that made them great friends. But there was a growing divide here. Laura was beginning to feel as if she was standing between two completely different worlds — two friends — and almost having to choose between them.

Chapter Six

Laura left her room in search of her parents, and found them huddled over a final guest list of people who would be attending the Bat Mitzvah party. They were immersed in trying to decide whom they would seat next to whom at the dinner.

"But Gary, we can't seat your Uncle Lou next to my cousin Anne," Laura's mother was saying. "Don't you remember that time your uncle insulted my cousin by telling her that he had become sick from the muffins she baked for our last family picnic? He said she tried to poison him. They haven't spoken since."

"Well, there's no one else to put him with, Lisa," her father replied. "So they'll have to pretend they like each other for the night."

Laura plunked herself down in between her parents, waiting for a lull in the conversation.

"What is it, Laura?" her mother finally asked. "You've looked unhappy for a couple of days now. Are you getting nervous about your Hebrew studies? I know there's a lot to learn, but you can't let it get to you."

Laura shook her head. "No, Mom, I keep telling you — that part's fine. It's just this twinning project and the book that Mrs. Mandelcorn gave me." By now, Laura had told her mother about receiving the diary, but little else.

Laura's parents waited expectantly. That was the great thing about them, Laura realized. Her parents never pushed her to talk when she was troubled. They let her take the lead, waiting until she was ready and then putting aside everything, just like now, to be there and listen.

Laura began to talk about Sara, her parents, grandmother, and siblings. "I don't know much about the Warsaw Ghetto. I'm just starting to find out some stuff about it." Laura's research had begun. She had already gone online, trying to find out some facts about the ghettos in Europe during the war — when they were formed, how, and what had happened there. Suddenly, the additional work seemed so important. When had Laura moved from feeling this was a burden, to feeling it was necessary?

"I knew that the ghettos were often built by the prisoners themselves," her father said. "There was a speaker at our synagogue last month; your mom and I went to hear him. His name is Henry Grunwald. He is a survivor of the Warsaw Ghetto and talked about how he and the other Jewish prisoners had to build the walls." Laura's father went on to talk about how the ghettos were constructed next to railway stations. "Mr. Grunwald said that at first, the ghettos were there just to keep Jews separate from their neighbors. But once the Nazis started taking Jews to the concentration camps, it was easy to collect them from the ghettos and load them onto the trains. I never knew that before."

Laura nodded. She didn't yet know what was going to happen to Sara, but already she had a sense of foreboding about the outcome of her story. Things could only get worse.

"Mr. Grunwald's talk was so moving. Gary, do you remember when he talked about the revolt in the ghetto?" her mother asked before turning to Laura. "They called it the Warsaw Ghetto uprising."

Laura interrupted. "I know. I've been reading about that too." It was late in the war and most of the Jews from the ghetto had already been deported to the death camps. But there was a secret underground organization of young Jewish fighters who banded together to fight back with whatever they had — a few guns, handmade bombs, and grenades.

"They were so badly outnumbered," her father continued. "One small group of fighters against an entire Nazi army. The Jews were bound to lose. But miraculously, the battle actually lasted for several weeks. The Nazis never expected the Jews in the ghetto to fight against them."

Laura's mother continued with the story. "You can imagine how humiliating it was when a handful of inadequately equipped, poorly trained young Jewish men and women were able to slow down the plans that the Nazis had in place for deportation. The Nazis finally set fire to what was left of the ghetto. The Jewish fighters were unbelievably courageous, right up until the end."

Silence hung in the air as Laura tried to digest what her parents were telling her. She already thought Sara was courageous, and she had barely begun to find out about her life.

"There are so many things I just don't understand about what happened during the war," Laura finally said. "I thought I knew this stuff from the project I did last year, but I really don't."

"It's hard for any one of us to understand how these things happened, Laura," her father replied. "Jews became scapegoats for Germany and the troubles it was experiencing after World War I. But that's not what you're looking for, is it?" he asked. Laura shook her head. She didn't want historical information about the events leading up to World War II. She wanted more than that. She wanted to know what Sara seemed to be asking — why the world had stood by and allowed these events to unfold in the first place.

"This project is becoming important to you, isn't it, honey?" her mother asked gently.

Laura nodded. "Nix doesn't understand. She thinks I'm an idiot for not being more excited about my dress right now."

Her mother nodded. "You and Nix are good friends. You'll find a way to work that out."

Laura nodded again. She kissed her parents good night and

retreated back to her bedroom. There was an e-mail from Nix waiting for her on her computer. *I don't get it,* the e-mail said. *Why are you more interested in some girl who lived a million years ago?*

Laura stared at the computer screen. She didn't feel like answering Nix. As she got ready for bed, Laura's head was clouded with questions and uncertainty. Perhaps she would never understand why things had happened as they did during the war. The one thing she did know was that she had finally made a commitment to the twinning project. And if her best friend couldn't understand how she felt about Sara and her life, well that was too bad.

Laura turned off her computer without answering Nix's e-mail. When her books were put together for the next day, Laura finally climbed into bed. Only then did she reach for the leather-bound diary, and opening it, she began to read.

November 9, 1941

David went out again last night, and this time he didn't return until the sun was coming up. I don't know where he goes and he doesn't say much. I've tried to ask him. But he just shrugs his shoulders and mumbles, "Just out."

I know there's more to it than that. I know there are groups of people organizing to fight back against the Nazis. David doesn't know it, but I overheard him once. He was in the courtyard of our building with his friends, Luba and Josef. David didn't see me standing behind the door. And that's when I heard them talking.

"We are strong. There are more and more of us each day," David was saying. "Soon we'll have enough to be able to do something."

I didn't know who "we" were, or what kind of action he was talking about. There was no Jewish army here in the ghetto.

"We've already managed to sneak some Jews out," David continued. "We've gathered arms and ammunition. It won't be long before we put these things to good use." David lowered his voice and looked around. I shrank back into the shadow of the doorway and strained to hear what he was saying.

"There will be another transport soon," whispered Josef. "We won't sit by and watch our brothers and sisters be taken away. We'll fight."

"There are not enough of us." Luba was talking now. "And what will we fight with? Twenty rifles won't stand up to one of their tanks."

"I'd rather die fighting here in the ghetto than be taken away," said David.

With that, David turned and started to walk back through the courtyard. I must have made a noise, stumbled on a loose brick because David caught me hiding behind the door. At first he was angry at me for eavesdropping on his conversation, but I didn't care. That's when I told him I wanted to help him with whatever he and his friends were planning. David wouldn't hear of it.

"You're a kid," he said. "Way too young. And you have no idea of the dangers out there."

"But if you can do something, then why can't I?" I demanded. "Besides, I'm twelve. If I'm old enough to be here, then I'm old enough to

Jewish resistance fighters could be stopped and arrested by the Nazis.

help. I can do whatever you do." Where did I get the courage to confront David like that? It's something Deena would have done, but not me!

Even David looked surprised at my outburst and stared at me a long time before answering. "What do you think you're going to do? Smuggle guns into the ghetto? Just last week, my friend, Jakob, was caught with a pistol on Chlodna Street. He probably didn't even see the military car that pulled up behind him. He was dead in an instant." David stepped closer to me. "I won't let you do something so dangerous."

That's when I ran back upstairs. I didn't want to hear anymore. I didn't want to hear about people being shot. I didn't want to hear that there would be a transport out of the ghetto. And I didn't want to hear that my brother and others were going to fight with guns against Nazi tanks.

Sara Gittler

November 26, 1941

I know about transports and deportation. I know what the words mean. "Deportation: to be banished or exiled from your home and sent to an unknown destination." I once looked it up in the dictionary. And I, like everyone in the ghetto, have heard the rumors about where Jews are being sent. You have to live with your head buried in the sand not to be aware of the news that sweeps through here. Deena and I sometimes talk about it.

"Those prisons in the east," I said one day as we sat on the stairs in front of my apartment. "Do you think they're as bad as everyone says they are?" Deena and I were tossing an old ball back and forth. David had pulled the ball out from a pile of garbage one day, and he had given it to me — one of those rare gestures that told me he still sort of cared about me, even if he didn't say so. The ball was almost in shreds; the top layer was hanging by a thread. But David covered it in cloth, and wrapped it in some chicken wire that he also found. So it was fine, and it gave me and Deena something to do besides just sit and watch the miserable people walk by.

Deena tossed the ball from one hand to the other as she thought about my question. "Rumors are a dangerous thing," she finally said. "We can't know what's true and what's exaggerated."

Sometimes, I think that Deena knows more than she lets on, just like my parents, and just like David. Deena is my age, but sometimes she thinks she needs to protect me from things, as if I can't handle the truth as well as she can. Deena knows me well, and sometimes I'm grateful that she doesn't talk about the things that she knows — like when she tells me she's in a hurry to draw everything she sees in the ghetto. But this time, I pushed her to say more.

"They say that Jews who are being deported are being killed in those prisons," Deena said slowly. "They say we're better off here in the ghetto, and that to be transported away is a death sentence."

I had never imagined that this horrible place could be a better alternative to anything. But Deena's words made me shiver uncontrollably. And it reminded me of something. "Do you remember when Mordke's parents were arrested?" I asked. Mordke was a boy my age who lived in a crowded flat with his parents and two other families. I used to stand with him by the gate, waiting for his parents and my Tateh to return to the ghetto after working in the factories on the outside. One day, Mordke's father tried to sneak some food past the guards at the gate. He had somehow managed to find or steal a head of cabbage that he tried to hide inside his coat. But the guards were searching everyone that day, and when they found the cabbage they beat Mordke's father and threw him on a truck. I thought that Mordke was going to charge the guards, and I had to hold him back so he wouldn't be beaten along with his father. Mordke struggled in my arms but I held him tightly and told him to be quiet. When Mordke's mother tried to help her husband she was also thrown on the truck. Just like that! Mordke's parents were arrested and taken away, and Mordke was left to fend for himself in the ghetto. It was so sad to see him all alone after that, begging on the streets just like the old sick people. Mama often brought him into our home to share what little food we had.

"Here's the thing," I said as I grabbed the ball from Deena's hands and turned her to face me. "We've all felt so sorry and sad for Mordke. He's here all alone in the ghetto. But at least he's still here. Maybe the people we should feel sad about are his parents."

Deena just stared at me. She had no response, and in that moment, I realized the rumors must be true.

Sara Gittler

December 19, 1941
Freezing cold! My fingers and toes are numb. I am sitting indoors, under a blanket. No heat.

Sara Gittler

January 12, 1942
Tateh took me to visit the orphanage today. He knows the man who runs it. His name is Janusz Korczak. "He's a great man," Tateh says. "A generous human being." Tateh used to teach at the orphanage; that's how he came to know Mr. Korczak. Actually, he is really Dr. Korczak, but he gave up his medical practice when he decided to devote his life to taking care of orphans. He even once ran a home for Catholic orphans and dreamed of creating a place where Catholic and Jewish children could live together. That's what Tateh told me. Isn't that a lovely idea? Children of different religions living together like brothers and sisters. It's the way things ought to be. Of course, it never happened. In fact, eventually Dr. Korczak wasn't allowed to be the director of the Catholic orphanage because he was Jewish. And when the ghetto was created he decided to stay here with the Jewish children he was taking care of.

I hadn't wanted to go with Tateh to the orphanage. I was feeling particularly hungry that morning. It isn't fair that there is so little to eat in the ghetto. There was a time long before the war when our icebox was so full that when you opened the door, it felt as if the food was going to leap out. These days, the cupboards echo with emptiness along with my stomach. Here is what we get to eat in the ghetto. There is one midday meal from the central kitchen, but I wouldn't call it a meal at all; it's really just a bowl of watery soup with a few vegetables floating on top. The ration card that Tateh has gets us 800 grams of bread a month and 250 grams of sugar. With that we get a few potatoes and sometimes some cabbage or beets; if we're lucky, a few grams of jam. And that's it! Mama barters for other things like a soup bone, or a few grams of cheese. But there is less and less to barter with. Soon, she will have to start pulling up wooden slats from the apartment floor!

People had to line up at the central kitchen for the midday rations.

I long for just one of Mama's meals that she used to make in our old home — one plate of roast brisket with sweet potatoes and carrots. In those days, I used to eat meals with hardly a thought about what I was putting in my mouth. These days, eating the little food we have is something that requires concentration. Each bite is deliberate; each mouthful memorable.

"Stop feeling so sorry for yourself, Saraleh," said Tateh. That's when he said I had to go with him to the orphanage. "Dr. Korczak is a friend of mine," he said. "I want to talk to him about doing some teaching again at the orphanage. It will be good for my soul," Tateh added.

I didn't know what that had to do with me or why I had to go along.

"Perhaps this will put your life in some perspective," Tateh said, though I didn't quite know what that meant.

Tateh and Dr. Korczak were happy to see one another and embraced like long lost friends. I stared at Dr. Korczak. He is tall and thin and has a head as round and bald as a full moon. The children stood in quiet rows behind the doctor — about twenty of them. The oldest was about twelve, the youngest no more than four or five. Their eyes were curious.

"Stay here with the children," Tateh told me. "I'm going to talk with Janusz. I won't be long."

As soon as Tateh left with Dr. Korczak, I was surrounded by a group of boys and girls. Most of them could not have been more than Hinda's age, and I felt sadder than when I had left my cat behind before coming to the ghetto. These children had no parents, no grandparents to look after them and to love them. Not only were they here in this horrible ghetto, but they were completely alone. And yet, they did not seem unhappy at all. In fact, Bubbeh looked sadder than these young children, and she had all of us!

The children tugged on my hand, wanting me to come with them and play. I followed them into a larger room where they surrounded me with looks of such expectation that I suddenly had an idea.

Janusz Korczak cared for the children in the orphanage.

Some girls sewed clothing in the orphanage.

Boys and girls had lessons, worked in the garden, and put on plays and concerts.

"All right, everyone," I said. "Sit down and I'll tell you a story."

The children plunked themselves down at my feet and I began to tell them the legend of the trumpeter of Krakow.

There was a watchman who stood guard in the tallest tower in the city of Krakow — the Mariacki Church of Saint Mary. This watchman would blow his trumpet if he believed that the city was in danger.

One night, the watchman saw a group of invaders approaching. He blew his trumpet to alert the townspeople. The invaders shot arrows at him in the tower, but he continued to blow the trumpet until he was hit in the throat by an arrow.

Eventually, the invaders were forced back, the city was saved, but the watchman died from his wounds.

Since that time, a trumpeter always plays a little hymn in Krakow, repeating it every hour. It ends on a high note to honor the watchman who died protecting his city.

As I told the story, one little boy's face caught my attention. He had dark hair, dark eyes, and freckles across his nose just like me. His eyes grew so round as I told my story that I thought they would pop out of his face. I was just finishing up when Tateh and Dr. Korczak entered the room.

"That one will certainly grow up to be a fine teacher, like you," said Dr. Korczak, pointing at me while Tateh smiled approvingly.

Before leaving, I said good-bye to the children, pausing to speak to the little boy with the freckles.

"Did you like my story?" I asked. He nodded. "What's your name?"

"Jankel," he said. "Will you come back? Will you come and tell us another story?"

"I'll try," I said, reaching down to give him a hug before following Tateh out the door.

"It was a good thing you did, Saraleh," said Tateh. "These poor children have nothing. If it weren't for Janusz, who knows what would happen to them? He finds them food and clothing and beds to sleep in. There are even activities and plays that Janusz organizes for the children. Imagine, here in this squalor, these children are able to play."

I was quiet on the walk back to the apartment, thinking about what Tateh had said. That morning I had felt like the unfortunate one. I had so little to eat, and no new clothes, and a cramped room that I shared with my grandmother. But compared with these children, I felt as if I had all the riches in the world. I had my parents, Bubbeh, Hinda, and even David, whether or not he talked to me. It was amazing how one person's misfortunes could suddenly make your own life seem so much better. I vowed right then and there to return to the orphanage whenever I could.

Sara Gittler

January 16, 1942

Yesterday, David left the house without his armband. That's against the law and you can be arrested or even shot if you are caught without one on. Everyone must wear the white armband with the blue Star of David whenever we are outside. I hate my armband. It's like a vice wrapped around my arm, squeezing tighter and tighter, reminding me that I am different. We have to make our own armbands, or buy them from the boy on the street who walks around carrying dozens of them on a stand. Mama refuses to pay for the armbands. She says it's just like

Everyone in the ghetto had to wear a
white armband with a blue Star of David.

Jews made their armbands
or bought them from vendors
on the street.

the construction of the ghetto. "The men built the prison and now the women have to buy the prison uniforms. Ridiculous!" she says. So instead, Mama, Bubbeh, and I sew them by hand. It gives Bubbeh something to do, something to keep her mind off her sadness.

I saw David's armband lying on his cot. So I ran after him to tell him he wasn't wearing it. I thought maybe he had just forgotten. Well, I should have known better. When I caught up with David around the corner from our apartment, he turned around and hissed at me to leave him alone and get back inside.

I didn't want to tell Mama and Tateh, didn't want to worry them. So I sat on David's cot and rocked back and forth. Mama thought I might be sick and she kept pressing her lips to my forehead to see if I had a fever. The truth is I was sick with fear for David's safety.

He came back late that night, and you won't believe this. When David opened his coat, food fell out from the inside! There were two bunches of carrots, a head of cabbage, and some onions. He even had a bag with sugar and one with flour that he pulled from his pockets. It was as if a treasure had fallen from the sky; that's how incredible this was! Mama threw herself at David, hugging him and squealing with delight. But in the next minute, I thought she was going to throttle him.

People tried to smuggle food into the ghetto.

We didn't know what he had done to get the food, but we knew it must have been ridiculously dangerous.

Later that night, when everyone was sleeping, I went to David's cot and I asked him point-blank how he had gotten everything. At first, he didn't want to tell me. But I just stood there and waited. I think I have a right to know these things. And finally, David began to talk. He told me that there is a way to get out of the ghetto — holes in the walls that some of the Jews have created. David crawled through one of these holes and went scavenging for food.

"I went back to the old market close to our house" said David. Mr. Novakowski was still there, selling his goods as if nothing had changed in the world. When he saw me walk into his store, I thought he'd have a heart attack." David would have been arrested on the spot if he, a Jew, was seen on the streets of Warsaw. But we both knew that Mr. Novakowski might also be punished if he was seen talking to a Jew. "That was my one advantage," continued David. "I thought Mr. Novakowski would do anything to get me out of there as quickly as possible. He shoved all this stuff into my hands and I disappeared as quickly as I could."

David said that the hardest part was walking back to the ghetto. "It was like a taste of freedom," he said. "Better than all the vegetables I carried in my pockets."

Listening to David talk about being on the outside of the ghetto walls was more than I could ever imagine. I was light-headed just thinking about it. "Take me with you!" I blurted the words before I had a chance to think. "The next time you go out — take me with you." I didn't even think about the danger. "Please, David," I pleaded. "I have to do something. I'm small," I added. "I could crawl in places you couldn't get to."

David stopped. For a moment I thought he might snap at me again, tell me to leave him alone, tell me I'm too young to get involved. But this time he didn't. And after a moment, he said, "I'll think about it."

The next day, we feasted on a stew that Mama made. She even put in a meat bone that she had been saving for a special occasion. My stomach felt fuller than it had in weeks. But the best part was that David actually said I might be able to help him. Wouldn't that be the greatest irony — if the ghetto brought David and me closer together?

Sara Gittler

Since they could not go to school,
children played on the streets.

Chapter Seven

When she went to the breakfast table the two days later, Laura was rubbing her eyes, trying to clear away the exhaustion. It wasn't from reading the journal, though she had done that late into both nights. It was that after putting the diary down, she had been unable to fall asleep — each time. She had closed her eyes, she had tried to take deep breaths, she had tried to focus on other things — *happy thoughts*, her mother used to call them. But it was no use. Try as she might, Laura couldn't stop thinking about Sara, her family, the threat of deportation, the orphanage she had visited. Laura felt as if she were on a roller-coaster, holding on for dear life as her mind sped through the events of Sara's life. Hours went by each night as Laura continued to toss and turn.

Last night had been the worst. When she finally fell asleep, Laura began to dream. She imagined that she and Emma were marching in a long line of children. It was nighttime, or at least it seemed that way; the sky was black and a thick mist hung in the air like stale smog on a cloudy humid day. Her parents were nowhere in sight and Laura looked everywhere to find them, searching left and right, in front of her and behind her. It was no use. She and Emma were all alone, orphans in a sea of children. She clutched Emma's hand knowing that she mustn't let go; to let go would be to lose the last thread, the last connection to a family member. Someone pushed her roughly from behind and she turned to face a man with an ugly, leering stare. He opened his mouth and shouted, "Jew!" in Laura's direction. The sound bounced and echoed in the thick air and as Laura stumbled forward, she tripped and her fingers slipped away from her sister's hand. "Emma!" she screamed but the sound of her voice was lost in the thickness of the smoke that swallowed her. That's when Laura woke up.

Sweat poured from her brow and her throat felt dry and tight as if she were choking on something she had eaten. Dreams were worse than stories, Laura realized. You couldn't put them down, put them aside until you were ready to deal with them. Dreams crept up on you when you weren't looking, and they held you in their grip. If she were three or four years old, Laura would have headed promptly for her parents' bedroom and there, in the safety of her mother's arms, she would have found peace and comfort. But Laura had long outgrown that childish ritual. Instead, she lay awake in her bed, haunted by the nightmarish images, until the early morning light began to seep into her room through the shades in the window, and she could hear her parents getting up and preparing for the day.

Laura lay still for a few minutes longer. Emma was awake and padding through the hallway, reminding her mother that she had promised to bring cookies for all the children in her class. This is crazy, Laura thought. She had to stop feeling so connected to Sara's stories, stop letting them get to her. What was it about the diary that had this powerful hold on Laura? She still couldn't answer that. All she knew was that something was propelling her forward, deeper and deeper into Sara's life.

By the time Laura got to the kitchen table, her mother had managed to scrounge up a bag of cookies for Emma who was now happily eating breakfast and going on and on about the leaves she had collected for a school project.

"It's my very important work," Emma said, a serious frown creasing her forehead.

In between responding to Emma, Laura's parents were reading the newspaper — their morning ritual — dividing the sections and passing them back and forth. Laura grabbed a slice of toast and a glass of orange juice and sat down. Quickly, she reached for a section of the paper and buried her head behind it, hoping her parents wouldn't notice her red puffy eyes and pale skin. She had tried slapping cold water onto her face to bring some color back, but she knew there were some things she could never hide from her mom. She fully expected an interrogation.

Laura scanned the headlines, her eyes jumping from one article to the next, when something suddenly caught her attention and she stiffened. There in the middle of the page, black, bold letters nearly jumped out at her.

JEWISH CEMETERY VANDALIZED

"Laura, don't forget you've got an orthodontic appointment after school. So I need you to come straight home." Her mother was talking to her, but Laura didn't even hear what she was saying. "Laura, are you listening?"

Laura raised her head from the paper and stared at her mother.

"What is it?" her mother asked. "What's wrong?"

"Did you see this?" Laura spoke in a whisper. She placed the paper on the kitchen table where everyone could see it; she felt too stunned to say another word.

Laura's father picked up the newspaper and scanned it quickly. "It says here that a number of gravestones were knocked over and several of them broken in half." He read aloud from the newspaper article:

There are no immediate suspects, but the police believe that several teenagers might be responsible for the damage. They are asking for the public's help in providing information that might lead to the arrest of the young people who were involved in the crime.

"This is outrageous!" he said, looking up. His face was bright red.

Laura grabbed the paper back and continued to read. The article reported that the cemetery's director had discovered the damage when he arrived in the morning and he had reported the incident to the police. The authorities were describing this as a clear case of anti-Semitism, *a despicable act of hatred against the Jewish community.* There was even a quote by the mayor who said they were treating the episode seriously.

"This event will not be tolerated. I stand with our Jewish friends and with all decent citizens in condemning this senseless act. I call on the community to fight against anti-Semitism whenever and wherever it occurs."

There were photographs in the paper as well. One was a picture of a gravestone lying on its side and broken in two pieces. Someone — one of the vandals — had spray painted a *swastika* on the stone, covering the name of the deceased with bright red paint. Laura knew what the spray painting was. Adolf Hitler had adopted this emblem as the symbol of his Nazi party. All of those old photographs of Hitler always placed him in front of massive flags bearing the swastika. And when the Nazis had begun to prohibit Jewish citizens from entering restaurants, parks, and schools, they had left that same sign painted on shop windows and restaurant doors. The people who had sprayed the swastikas in the cemetery must have been filled with the same kind of hatred, Laura realized.

"I can't believe something like this could happen here," said Laura's mother.

"Mom?" Laura searched her mother's face for some reassurance. Even the usually chatty Emma was startled into silence. She had stopped eating and was staring at her parents, trying to absorb what she could of the conversation, aware that something serious was taking place.

"I know this is upsetting, but you mustn't worry, honey. It'll be fine," her mother replied. "The police will get whoever is responsible. We'll talk more about it later."

Laura was speechless. She knew this cemetery; it was close to her school and she passed it every day on the walk to and from. The paper had called it anti-Semitism — "acts of hatred against the Jewish community." That was scary enough. But scarier still was the realization that this wasn't 1939 and they weren't talking about Poland. This was taking place today in Laura's city — in her own neighborhood! The comparison with what she had been reading about Sara's life in Warsaw was just too overwhelming.

Chapter
Eight

Laura took the long way to school. She wanted to walk the full length of the cemetery and see for herself just what had happened. At first she couldn't see anything. The cemetery looked as peaceful as ever. Soft rolling green hills and giant trees cradled the gravestones that were lined up like rows of desks in Laura's classroom. But then she saw something, off in one corner and close to an exterior wrought iron fence — yellow police tape that was wrapped around several trees, surrounding one small section of the cemetery grounds. Laura moved closer to the fence and pressed her face between two of the black iron bars. She could see the gravestones that had been knocked over, the ones that were pictured in the newspaper. Even from this distance, the red painted swastikas glowed like neon signs at an amusement park.

Several police officers were still there, patrolling the area, making sure no one came close. A number of people stood off to one side. At first, Laura wondered if they were suspects. But as she looked closer, she realized that they must be family members whose loved ones were buried in the section of the cemetery that had been vandalized. Men and women stood with their arms around one another. Several were crying as they looked at the disaster in front of them. Laura couldn't imagine how painful this must be for them; first to lose a relative and then to see that relative's resting place destroyed and defaced in this terrible way. Despite the warmth in the morning air, Laura shivered uncontrollably.

By the time she reached the school, the grounds were full of students, all talking about the incident in the cemetery. Laura was looking for Adam and finally spotted him standing against the wall. He was wearing one of his many Beatles T-shirts, this one adorned with a picture of John Lennon and the message "Give Peace a Chance" written underneath.

"Did you hear about the cemetery?" Laura asked as she pushed through a crowd of students to stand next to her friend.

"Who hasn't heard?" Adam replied. "My parents were crazy this morning. They think the world's become evil! And the police are all over the school." Adam gestured toward the school steps and Laura followed his gaze. Two police officers were standing outside the front door of the school. They were stopping some of the students on their way in and talking to them intently.

"Why are they here?" Laura asked.

Adam shrugged. "The cemetery's practically next door to the school, and the newspaper article said that some kids had probably done it. I guess the police figure someone here might be involved."

"Did they arrest anyone?" Laura asked.

"I don't think so. I think they're just asking questions, trying to find anyone who might have seen what went on."

Laura and Adam paused to watch the activity around the school doors. "It's so weird," continued Laura. "Here I am reading this diary from a girl during the Holocaust. She talks about all these times when Jews were being discriminated against — horrible things like spray painting signs on restaurants and theaters for Jews to keep out. And then something like this takes place right here in our own neighborhood. Things like this aren't supposed to happen here." She paused to let this sink in.

"Hey, have you seen Nix?" Adam asked. The three of them usually met outside school about this time.

"Probably late, as usual," replied Laura, uneasily. She had avoided Nix for two days and wasn't sure she was ready to face her yet — wasn't certain how to talk to Nix after her e-mail two nights earlier. Anyway, the bell was about to ring and Laura needed to get to her own class.

With minutes to spare, she suddenly spied Nix walking slowly toward the school. Her eyes were on the police officers at the front door and she was so focused on the activity there that she nearly walked straight past Laura and Adam.

"Hey, we're over here," shouted Adam. Nix stopped short and darted a glance at Laura and then Adam. She waved hesitantly and then looked as if she might move on without stopping to talk.

"Wait up," said Adam. "What's the matter?"

"I . . . I've got to get to class," replied Nix.

"Since when did you care if you were on time?" asked Adam. There were times when he was frustrated with Nix's lateness as well. "Hey, did you hear about the cemetery?"

Laura hung back, still not sure what to say to Nix. She'd let Adam do the talking.

"Yeah, but it's no big deal," Nix replied, and turned to walk away.

"Are you kidding me?" blurted Laura. "It's huge. The police are looking for suspects."

Nix shrugged. "Some stupid kids, I guess."

"It's more than that!" Laura felt her cheeks flame and suddenly she had a lot to say. "They destroyed the graves. And painted swastikas all over them — Nazi signs. Didn't you see the newspaper?" This was more than Laura could cope with. She couldn't believe that Nix wasn't more disturbed by what had happened.

"Of course I saw it," snapped Nix. "So what? We didn't do anything, so why are you so freaked out?"

It was as if she were standing in front of a stranger. Laura's mouth fell open. "I'm upset because it's the Jewish cemetery. And they didn't just do some stupid things. They did horrible things to the graves of people — Jewish people. And I'm upset because I'm reading all this stuff about a Jewish girl in the war and nobody was there to help her and these kinds of things were happening to her and her family. And I'm upset because you don't seem to get any of it. That's why I'm freaked out!" Laura's voice was rising. How could Nix be so uncaring, so uninterested? "Doesn't it bother you that this happened?"

Nix shrugged again. She looked over at the police officers once more. "What do you think will happen if they catch the people who did it?"

"They'll go to jail, I hope," Laura replied.

"But nobody got hurt, did they?" Nix continued. "It's like when those grade nine boys broke the window at the back of the school. They paid for the damage and that was all that happened."

"But that was an accident, Nix. This was totally deliberate — and terrible." Nix's behavior was growing stranger and more disturbing by the minute.

"I've got to get to my class," Nix said as she moved away.

"Wait!" Laura said.

"I'm late," shouted Nix over her shoulder.

"Will you meet me at lunch?" As upset as she was by Nix's reaction, Laura felt that she needed to talk to her, to try and get her to understand the situation. But Nix had moved on and didn't turn around to respond to Laura.

"That was weird," said Adam finally. "What do you think is up with her?"

"It's like she doesn't care about anything important anymore." This was not like Nix. Nix was on the student council, she raised money for the homeless shelters in town, she rescued abandoned animals. Nix cared about things, cared about people. For her to ignore the enormity of this crime, or to suggest that it was unimportant, made no sense at all. Laura paused and reached up to rub her eyes. She was exhausted from lack of sleep and from the events of the morning. It all seemed so overwhelming — the incident in the cemetery, her friend's behavior, Sara's life — everything!

Chapter Nine

After school that day, Laura walked home with Adam. At lunch, she had tried to find Nix, but her friend was nowhere in sight. In the end, Laura ate her lunch alone, outside, on the steps of the school. From where she sat, she could see the cemetery down the street. Police cars were still in front and there appeared to be constant movement to and from the section where the graves had been vandalized. The officers had already left the school, but not before making an announcement over the intercom. They said that they were following up on some leads, but that they still needed the help of students who might know something about what had happened. "Any information, no matter how small or unimportant to you, might be critical to us," the officer said. Once the police had finished talking, Mr. Garrett spoke as well.

He urged students to come forward and help solve the crime.

Laura listened to it all with some detachment. She was still terribly disturbed by the vandalism in the cemetery. But more than that, she was upset by Nix's behavior. Why was Nix avoiding her and acting so bizarre? Why didn't she seem to care about the incident?

"So, what are you saying — that you think Nix did it?" asked Adam as they walked side by side past the cemetery once more. There was an eerie feeling in the air, as if the crime still hung there like a shroud.

"No! I don't know. Of course not!" Laura replied. It was impossible to imagine that Nix might be involved in some way. But what other explanation was there for the way she was acting? First there was her lack of interest in Sara's journal, and now she didn't seem to care about the vandalism. "You saw her this morning, Ad. She barely looked at us. And she asked all those questions about what would happen if they caught the person who did it. Then she made it sound as if the whole thing was unimportant."

"So you're saying it's kind of like those stories you hear about your sweet next door neighbor turning out to be a serial killer, or something like that," said Adam as he shifted his backpack from one shoulder to the other.

"Stop it! This isn't a joke." It was hard enough to think that Nix might be involved in the incident. Adam wasn't helping.

"So what are you going to do about it?" Adam asked.

Laura shook her head. "I have no idea. But I do know that I've got to talk to Nix and try to figure out what's going on." That's what was missing. Without a real conversation it all just became speculation and gossip, and that was a dangerous thing.

"Do you want me to do anything? Remember what John says. *'I get by with a little help from my friends.'*"

Laura shook her head and smiled. "Thanks. I'll let you know if anything happens."

Laura started telephoning Nix as soon as she got home from the orthodontist. At first, there was no answer and Laura didn't bother leaving a message. She just kept calling and calling until finally Nix's brother, Peter, answered the phone. "No . . . uh . . . she's not here," he said. "Hey, did you guys have a fight or something?"

"No," said Laura wearily. "Do you know where she is?"

"She's . . . um . . . out. Just out. I'll tell her you called." And with that he hung up.

Laura sat for another minute, still holding the phone, listening to the sound of the dial tone. This was getting stranger and more worrisome by the minute. Not only was Nix avoiding her at school, but now she was avoiding her on the phone. Laura knew that Nix must be at home and had probably put her brother up to lying for her. But why? For the next couple of hours, Laura sat staring at her homework, aware that there was so much work she needed to do, but unable to focus. The only thing she could think about was talking to Nix and trying to straighten this out. Nothing else mattered.

Eleven o'clock. Was it too late to call Nix again? Laura shook her head. I have to give it one last try, she thought as she picked up the telephone. When Nix answered on the fourth ring, Laura exhaled slowly.

"Hello." Nix's voice was small and timid on the other end, not at all like the confident person that she really was.

"Finally!" cried Laura. "What's happening, Nix?" She had wanted to be calm when Nix answered the phone, but all Laura could do was blurt out her frustration. "There's something going on. Talk to me — please!"

"It's nothing. Look, I'm really busy right now. I'll see you tomorrow — I promise."

Laura sensed that Nix was about to hang up, and she couldn't let that happen. This was her chance to confront her friend. Laura blurted into the telephone, "Did you do it? Is that why you won't talk to me?"

There was silence. Had Nix hung up, or had she just frozen in the face of Laura's accusation? Finally a small voice on the other end of the telephone replied, "Is that what you think — that I could actually *do* something like this?"

"Well, you're acting all weird and you won't say anything. Yesterday, you didn't care about the diary that I'm reading. And today you don't seem to care that this horrible thing happened. What am I supposed to think?" Laura could begin to feel hot tears rising behind her eyes, but she shook them away. She didn't want to cry. And yet she felt dangerously close to discovering something about her best friend that she didn't want to know. It scared her.

Finally, Nix spoke. "I could never do something like this. Don't you know that? And yes, I think it's horrible too."

"Then what is the matter with you? Why have you been acting like this?"

Once again there was silence on the other end of the phone. Laura clutched the receiver, praying silently that her friend would open up to her. And then finally, after what seemed like an eternity, Nix spoke softly. "I saw them."

"What?" For a moment Laura wasn't sure what Nix was saying.

"I saw them — the boys who did it. There were three of them. They go to our school. They're in grade nine. You know who they are." There was another long pause. "They're the same guys who Adam bumped into last week." Nix took a deep breath and continued. "I was leaving school late yesterday because of the student council meeting and I thought I'd take the shortcut through the cemetery. I had just gotten to this huge tree close to the fence when I saw those same three guys by the gravestones. They looked like they were doing something wrong, so I hid behind the tree where they couldn't see me. I was scared. I kept thinking about what they had said to Adam. I kept thinking about how they had threatened him, about how they bully everyone.

"I figured I would just wait until they left, and then I would get home. That's when I saw one of them pull out the spray can. The two other guys knocked over the stones, and the third one did the spray painting." Nix went on to describe how she had watched, terrified from behind the tree, not knowing what to do, praying that they wouldn't see her. "They finally took off, and I ran out of there so fast. I didn't look back, not for a second."

Laura sat listening to the whole story with her eyes shut tight, as a mixture of emotions exploded inside her. Relief! Nix had not committed the crime after all. Fear! Her friend might have been hurt if she had been discovered spying. Anger! Why had Nix felt as if she couldn't confide in her? "Were you going to tell me?" she finally asked.

"I'm telling you now."

"Only because I made you!"

There was another long moment of silence. "Why does it matter so much?" Nix asked finally.

Laura took a deep breath. Nix still didn't seem to understand. "You're a witness," Laura said.

"I know," Nix replied.

"Well, you've got to tell someone — your parents, the police."

"No way!" shouted Nix. "Those guys could be expelled from school for this. They could get arrested. Don't you get it? If one of those guys finds out I'm the one who told on them, they could come after me."

"But you're the one who told Adam to stand up to them." Laura was fighting to stay calm.

"I know," said Nix. "But it's so different when you're the one being threatened."

"You have to say something," insisted Laura. "You can't turn your back and pretend it didn't happen."

"This is why I didn't want to tell you." Nix's voice was rising on the other end of the telephone. "I'm not getting involved in this. Let the police figure it out on their own."

Laura was having difficulty controlling both the rapid beating of her heart and her rising anger. But she had to remain composed if she was going to convince Nix to speak up about the incident. "Do you remember when that little boy went missing from his home last month, and we tried to talk our parents into taking us out to join the search for him?" Everyone had feared the worst for the four-year-old — that he had been kidnapped, or even killed. Luckily, he had been found sleeping in a nearby park. He had been playing hide and seek with some friends and wandered away to hide. When no one came to get him, he had fallen asleep and was found by a search party hours later. That incident also made the front page of the paper. "You and I couldn't wait to get involved then," said Laura.

"That was different," Nix replied. "There was a whole group of people trying to help one little kid. I'm the only witness here. I'm all alone. You don't understand what that's like. I just can't do it. So leave me alone." With that, Nix finally slammed down the receiver.

Laura quietly replaced the phone and then slumped down onto her bed, holding her head in her hands. Nix was a coward — and selfish. She was only thinking about herself and not about the families who had been affected by this crime, the community — Laura's community — that had been attacked. That's what it felt like. Laura was feeling as if the destruction in the cemetery was an attack on her people — on her personally. And by refusing to come forward and report the crime, it was as if Nix were turning her back on her. Nix had let her down.

Laura moved to her desk and looked at her pile of homework. There was so much she needed to do, but it was late and she was exhausted. And then there was Sara's journal. Laura still had no idea what she was going to do for this project, but the clock was ticking and her Bat Mitzvah was around the corner. There was too much to think about and yet, Laura believed that everything that had happened today in the cemetery and with Nix was linked to Sara's life in some way. She reached for the diary and, brushing her hair behind her ears, she opened it and continued to read.

March 14, 1942

Deena and I went out to steal bread today. It wasn't really my idea — or Deena's for that matter. It was Mendel's, the boy who lives in the flat below mine. He is fourteen — taller than I am. He was bragging that he knew how to sneak into the back of the building where the Nazis store food. He told us that just a week earlier he had stolen three loaves of freshly baked bread for his family. Three whole loaves! Just two weeks ago, I lined up in front of the bakery for four hours just to try and get a few stale slices. By the time I got to the front of the line, all the bread was gone, and I came home empty-handed.

Many Jewish families had once gone to
The Great Synagogue on Tlomacki Street.

Mendel brags a lot, like the time he told me he had snuck out of the ghetto through a sewer, or about how his father still owns a radio even though it's forbidden. I'm never quite sure whether to believe him or not. But he promised to show Deena and me the way to steal bread, so we agreed to go with him. I wouldn't dare tell Mama where I was going. She would have forbidden it. So I said I was going to Deena's and would be back soon. I think Deena told the same lie to her parents. I can't wait around forever for David to let me help him. I need to do something to show him I can be useful. I knew that getting bread for the family would prove to him that I wasn't a baby.

It was cold and damp outside. My jacket is quite warm but it is far too small for me. The sleeves only reach three-quarters of the way down my arms, and the buttons pull across my chest. I don't know what I will wear if we're still here next winter. By then, the jacket will only be good enough for Hinda. But for now it's all I've got. Mama complains all the time that I am growing too fast.

We met Mendel a few blocks away in front of the Great Synagogue on Tlomacki Street. Before the war, my family used to go to religious services in that synagogue. As a child, I was always amazed at its big domed roof and massive stone pillars. I felt tiny next to the grandeur of the synagogue. Now of course, it's just another empty, neglected building.

I hate walking alone through the ghetto. There are so many sick and dying people on the street. Some are there just to beg for food, but many have no place to live and the gutters have become their home. They hold their hands outstretched, and their eyes are haunted and hollow. Often, these sick people die right there in the street, still holding their arms straight out in front of them like statues; on their faces, an expression of complete shock, as if they have suddenly realized that have been completely abandoned. The carts go by twice a day to pick up the dead bodies and take them away. I don't know where they are taken, and Tateh won't tell me. I don't think these old sick Jewish men and women will have a proper burial like my Zaideh had when he died. There will be no rabbi there to say prayers at their grave; no family members to remember them, and talk about the good things they did in their lives. The bible says that Jews are the chosen people. Well, right now, I think we are the forgotten people!

It was hard to walk past people begging for food on the street.

There have been a few outbreaks of typhoid fever in the ghetto. That's the other reason my parents are so worried when I am outside. Typhoid fever is caused by eating food or drinking water that is dirty. It's next to impossible to find any water that's clean in the ghetto, and in our flat, Mama tries to boil the water to rid it of as many germs as possible.

The smells in the ghetto are unbearable. I practically gag and have to hold my sleeve across my nose. The gutters are filthy and attract rats that have made their homes here alongside the Jews. The rats carry fleas and other diseases, and they have become so bold that they will come right up to you. They are starving along with the rest of us, and they almost taunt you with their sharp eyes and sharper teeth. As Deena, Mendel, and I wound our way through the ghetto streets, I tried to stare straight ahead and not breathe in. And I walked quickly to avoid stepping on a rat.

Mendel led the way, turning left and right, walking so quickly that Deena and I had to run to keep up. I thought of turning back several times, but I think that Deena sensed I might abandon the plan. So she held onto my arm tightly, and wouldn't let go. She's much more adventurous than I am. That's one of the reasons I love having her as a friend. She pushes me to do things I might not ordinarily do. Like the time she convinced me to try out for that play in school. I never would have done it without her, and I ended up loving every minute of the experience. Deena is my bold side, and I am her reasonable one. But this time, in the back of my head, I kept thinking about David. If I'm going to do something to help his "cause," then I have to be bold. I have to put aside my fears, real or imagined. So Deena and I stumbled after Mendel until even Deena began to look worried.

"Mendel, stop!" she commanded, as we turned the twentieth corner. "Where are you taking us? This isn't a trick, is it?"

"Just follow me and be quiet," Mendel shouted over his shoulder and kept on walking. And that's what we did, until finally Mendel began to slow down. And then he turned to face us. "Crouch down and stay close to this wall," he said. "The storage building is right up there."

He pointed in front of him, and, sure enough, there was a small building up ahead. Its back door was wide open and as we watched, a man entered carrying a sack on his back.

"That's the bread," whispered Mendel. "He's bringing loaves in for the soldiers. He'll leave them in the back of the building while he goes to get more supplies. As soon as he's gone, we'll sneak in and take the bread."

Mendel made it sound so simple, but I knew it wasn't. What if someone saw us? What if we got caught? There were so many things that could go wrong — so many people who might see us. There were Jewish police who patrolled throughout the ghetto. Sometimes they were worse than the Nazis. The Jewish police gained favors for themselves and their families by working for the Nazis. If the Nazis caught us, they'd kill us for sure. If the Jewish police caught us, they'd hand us over to the Nazis. Either way, we would be doomed.

I looked over at Deena but she wouldn't meet my eyes. So I took a deep breath and thought of Bubbeh and Hinda. I was going to get food for my family. I was going to prove to David that I could do something more than sit around. Those thoughts were more important than any danger I imagined. So I followed Mendel as he darted over to the open door and glanced inside. A moment later, he turned and signaled for Deena and me to stay put. Then he disappeared inside the building. I held my breath, counting the seconds and wondering if Mendel would reappear or we would be abandoned and have to make our way back to our apartment. And then, finally, his head popped out from the back door like a jack in the box. He had a big grin on his face, and he held two

Anyone could be caught stealing.

loaves of bread in his arms like trophies. Triumphantly, Mendel tossed the loaves to Deena and me. Then he motioned that he was going back inside for more. A second later, he disappeared.

I clutched the loaf of bread in my arms like it was a treasure. And you can't even begin to imagine how heavenly the smell was. It overwhelmed me, hypnotized me. For a moment I was tempted to shove the whole thing into my mouth. David was right; when it comes to stealing food, the hardest part was not eating it right then and there. But I kept telling myself that the food was for my family. Mama and Tateh would be thrilled — that is, after they got past their fury that I had gone out to do this. I wasn't going to worry about that now. Surely their joy at having this unexpected treasure would replace any anger they would have.

I actually thought we had gotten away with it. I smiled that kind of smile over at Deena that says: We've just shared a great adventure and I'm glad we did it. But suddenly, my excitement disappeared as I heard the shrill whistle pierce the air along with the sound of police shouting from the other side of the storage building.

A second later, Mendel reappeared, and this time even he looked afraid. "Run!" he shouted as he took off down the street. For one second I froze, and then Deena grabbed my arm and we sprinted after Mendel. A chorus of shouts and whistles followed us as we rounded one corner after another. But I never looked back. Any second, I expected gunshots to ring out. I expected the police or the Nazis, or whoever was behind us, to overtake us, and right then and there, it would be over. But in the meantime, I followed Deena as we ran for our lives.

Suddenly I stumbled, and fell against Deena, almost knocking her glasses off her face. As I desperately reached out to grab Deena, both of our loaves of bread went flying out of our hands. Deena hesitated for one second, as if she was actually going to stop and retrieve her bread. But I pulled her along and we kept running.

A few minutes later, the whistles and shouts stopped. Deena and I ran on and on until we thought we were safe, and only then did we stop. By now, Mendel was nowhere in sight, and it took a long time to find our way back to our homes.

I never told my parents about our adventure, although I did tell David. He nodded and he looked at me with newfound respect. Maybe I proved something to him after all. I didn't speak to Mendel for days after that. I don't know what I was angrier about — that we had nearly been killed in this ridiculous scheme of his, or that we had failed and I had lost the bread.

I hope an old sick person from the gutter found the bread. I hope the rats didn't get it.

Sara Gittler

May 25, 1942

Today I did it! I became a soldier — and it was all thanks to David.

The truth is I had almost given up believing that I would be able to do anything useful here in the ghetto. I had given up hoping that David trusted me, believed in me enough to let me try and help. I had resigned myself to thinking that I would spend my days here only dreaming of fighting back, and that's all. But everything changed today.

When I woke up this morning I could tell that something was up with David. He was acting stranger than ever, pacing in the flat, looking at me from the corner of his eye, going to the window at least a hundred times. Even Bubbeh who is usually so consumed with herself, seemed to sense that David was acting odd. She walked over to him at one point and said, "Go outside, David. You are making me nervous here!"

That's when David finally stared straight at me. Our eyes locked and he nodded ever so slightly with his head, motioning me to follow him. We walked outside and into the courtyard, and there, David pulled me behind the door. When he was sure that no one else was around, he finally moved up close to me and said, "You say you want to do something, but are you really prepared to help?"

At first, I froze. Here I was, finally facing the opportunity I had been waiting for and I was almost too stunned to answer.

"Well, are you?" David's voice was getting louder and more urgent.

This time I nodded, but still couldn't speak.

That's when David told me what he wanted me to do. "We need a messenger," he said. "Someone small, someone who can move quickly and easily through the sewers." David went on to explain that there was a letter that had to be delivered to the outside. A contact was waiting beyond one of the gates of the ghetto. The contact would take the letter and then hand over one in return. David reached into his pocket and withdrew a small brown envelope. It was sealed and streaked with dirt; there was no writing on it. David turned it over in his hands and then looked at me. "I've gone out there too many times. I could be spotted. But your face is unknown. I'll show you where to go and tell you who to look for. You deliver this letter and bring me back the one that you're given. Do you understand?"

I stared at the letter and then at David. "What's in it?" I finally asked.

David shook his head. "The less I tell you, the better," he replied. "Just know that we are making contact with groups on the outside who are helping us with arms and information about the Nazis' plans. We've had couriers going back and forth for months now." Then his face softened. "It's okay to say no," he said. "It's okay if you're too scared. I'll understand."

I was scared — there was no doubt about that. I hadn't even begun this mission and my heart was pounding so hard, I thought David might even be able to hear it! But I knew I was ready to help. This time, I didn't need Deena to push me, or Mendel to dare me. I was ready on my own. I stared up at David and said, "Let's go."

And off we went, walking quickly through the ghetto streets, turning this way and that. This time I didn't even notice the people in the gutters. I didn't see the beggars by the side of the road. I stayed close on David's heels until he finally turned a corner onto a tiny deserted street. I didn't know where we were and it didn't really matter. David moved over to a sewer grate by the side of the road. He bent down and

The streets of the ghetto were crowded with people.

Children would smile, even though they were cold and hungry.

removed the grate. It made a high-pitched squealing sound — metal grating on metal. I glanced around. Would someone hear? There were small windowless buildings in this part of the ghetto and no one to watch us except a skinny old cat sleeping next to the gutter that picked up its head and stared in our direction.

"I'll be waiting here for you," David whispered. He shoved the letter deep into the pocket of my coat, looked around one more time, and then motioned me into the sewer. This was the moment. No time to think. I took a deep breath and descended into darkness.

If the smells were bad on the streets of the ghetto, they were almost unbearable inside the sewer — a mixture of waste and something rotting; I didn't even want to think about whether it was human or animal. I didn't want to think about what I might trip over. I plugged my nose and climbed down the small metal ladder leading from the opening into the bowels of the ghetto.

At the bottom, I looked around, waiting for my eyes to adjust to the shadows. David had said to go to the right, and that's where I went, avoiding the slimy walls, stepping carefully and quickly across puddles, rocks, and debris. At every fork in the tunnel I stayed to the right, remembering David's instructions. When the passage became too narrow, I crouched down low, careful not to bang my head on the jagged rocks above. No wonder they needed someone small, I thought. A grown man or woman would never have made it through the tiny openings.

How long was I in the sewers? Ten minutes? One hour? I had no idea of the passage of time. I kept moving forward, trying to stay calm, trying not to think about anything except David's instructions. When I saw the soft glow of light up ahead, I knew I was close to the opening and I quickened my pace.

There was a round hole at the end of the tunnel, filled with branches and rocks that had been placed there, David told me, to hide this opening. I peered through the gaps, glancing in each direction to make sure no one was watching. David had said that this part of the sewer came out behind an abandoned warehouse. The Nazis had not discovered this gap in the wall — at least not yet. No one in sight. Pushing aside the stones and branches, I climbed out of the sewer, pausing for a moment to brush off the dirt and dust from my coat and shoes. David had reminded me of that as well. "Clean away the evidence of the sewers," he had said. "You don't want to draw any suspicion."

Can a heart keep beating this fast before it explodes? I wondered as I rounded the corner of the abandoned warehouse and into the streets of Warsaw. I knew where I was — close to the corner of Zelazna and Grzybowska Street, in a small open square that my mother had walked me through hundreds of times before the war began and the walls were built. The streets were packed with people rushing in all directions. I wanted to stop and savor this moment of freedom. I wanted to throw my arms in the air and my head back, and breathe in the air on this side of the wall. But I couldn't do it. I suddenly felt as if a spotlight was on me. I looked and felt more Jewish than ever. Surely others would notice me — my dark hair and eyes, my sharp features. I shouldn't be here, I thought in a sudden panic. This mission was meant for someone else. I was certain that I was going to be arrested. The police would find the letter and trace it back to David and whoever else he was working with. This was a mistake!

My brain felt as if it was screaming out loud. That's when I looked around more carefully and could see that no one was interested in me. Men and women walked with their heads down, avoiding one another. The police at the corner strolled casually with their rifles slung over their shoulders. I had to calm down and finish what I had started.

I was looking for a woman in a green wool coat and green scarf. I spotted her easily, standing by a street lamp. Our exchange took seconds. "Excuse me. Do you know where the grocery store is on Nowolipki Street?" I asked. She nodded, acknowledging the question David had instructed me to ask. I withdrew the envelope and handed it to her. She handed me one in return. The exchange took seconds, and then she was gone, disappearing into the throng of nameless people on the streets of Warsaw.

I barely remember my trip back into the ghetto. All I remember is that I retraced my steps, as David had instructed and climbed out of the sewer to find my brother waiting for me. I handed him the envelope, he nodded, and then the two of us walked home.

No questions. No conversation. None was needed. But this much is true. I am different now, more grown-up, less afraid. I had always thought that freedom was about where you were. These ghetto walls had taken away every sense of freedom I ever had. But I suddenly realized that freedom was not just about where you were. Freedom was about who you were and who you chose to be. That day, when I completed the mission for David and the cause, I felt freer than ever before.

Sara Gittler

August 6, 1942

The most horrible thing happened today. It's almost too hard to write about it. But I have to. I have to see the words written down in front of my eyes to know it's true. This morning, the Nazis swept through the ghetto on a mission to arrest as many people as possible. They raided one apartment after another, pushing everyone out onto the streets and marching them to Umschlagplatz, the main square where they were going to get onto trains. It didn't matter if you were young, old, sick, or healthy. If your apartment was on their list, then you had to go. I watched out the window of our apartment, careful to stay behind the torn curtain, careful not to be seen.

But I did see Mordke on the street, the boy whose parents were arrested for sneaking food into the ghetto. And I saw Luba, David's friend, along with her parents, and others whom I knew and had spoken to almost every day since coming into the ghetto. All of them were standing on the street below my window, looking lost and afraid.

But that wasn't the worst of it. The worst was when I saw Deena walk out of her apartment building with her hands above her head and a Nazi rifle pressed into her back. Deena wasn't wearing her glasses.

She must have been forced from her apartment without even having a chance to put them on! As soon as I saw her lining up with her parents, my first thought was to run from my apartment down the stairs and out on the street. I wanted to throw myself in front of the Nazi soldiers and demand that they release Deena, and all the other Jews destined for deportation. But who was I kidding? There was nothing I could do to save Deena. Deena! My best friend! The one person with whom I had shared every important event in my life. What roll of the dice had determined that she was to be arrested while I, for the time being, was still safe? I could only watch helplessly as she and the others were marched down the street. I desperately wanted to shout to her. I wanted her to know that I saw her. I wanted to tell her to be brave and I wanted her to know that I'll keep her drawings — all of them, until she comes back to get them and she becomes a famous artist. I wanted her to hear me say that she is coming back.

An old man was pushed roughly from behind and he fell down hard on the pavement. His wife tried to pull him to his feet, screaming and wailing as if she was the one who had fallen. Then a young man tried to help, but a Nazi soldier was on him in a minute, punching him in the back with the butt of his rifle. Now there were two men on the pavement. Children were crying and grown-ups were screaming.

Suddenly, from around the corner, I saw Dr. Korczak, and behind him were all the children from the orphanage. I was filled with sadness that he and the children were also about to be taken away. I imagined that the children must be terrified and feeling even more alone than

Jews were rounded up and marched to Umschlagplatz for deporation.

ever. But a remarkable thing was happening. Unlike the screaming, crying people below, Dr. Korczak was marching calmly, taking slow, even steps. The children followed behind in rows of four across. They held their heads high and proud. At the front of the group, next to the doctor, was my little friend, Jankel. He was carrying the flag that had flown outside the door of the orphanage. It was green with white flowers on one side, and the Star of David on the other.

The people on the streets become silent as the crowd of children walked by. They moved aside, as Dr. Korczak passed. It was almost like Moses parting the waters of the Red Sea, though this time, the children were not being led to the Promised Land. They were being led to some terrible fate. And yet, no one cried. They marched with dignity and courage. It was the saddest and bravest thing I had ever witnessed.

That was when Tateh pulled me away from the window and wouldn't let me watch anymore. "There are some things that young eyes do not have to see," he said as he drew the curtain and led me into the kitchen. But I wanted to watch. Just like having to write these words on this page, I had to be a witness to what was happening to my friends. Only a few months earlier I had felt the excitement of doing something useful in the ghetto. When I had become a messenger for David I had felt hopeful and confident that maybe, just maybe, we could do more and more to drive the Nazis back. Now I felt the hope drain from my body.

"Where are the Nazis taking them, Tateh?" I asked.

Tateh winced and looked over at Mama. They exchanged that look that told me they knew the answer but they didn't want to tell me.

They were protecting me again, like some child. But I'm not a baby like Hinda. I've seen too much here already. You grow up fast in the ghetto and I've already seen more than most grown-ups in the outside world will ever see.

"Tell me, Tateh," I begged. "I need to know."

That's when David spoke up. Until then, he had sat in a corner with his head down. "They are going to the death camps!" he shouted.

The words just hung in the air, and suddenly I felt sick to my stomach.

Sara Gittler

Chapter Ten

"I'm so glad you called me, Laura," said Mrs. Mandelcorn. "At my age, I don't get many visitors. More cake?"

Laura was sitting in Mrs. Mandelcorn's living room. Two days had passed since the incident in the cemetery. The police had not yet been able to solve the crime and were still appealing to the public to come forward with information.

"The police think it happened in broad daylight," Laura's father had said the next morning. "Surely someone must have seen something — maybe someone from your school, kiddo?"

Laura had swallowed guiltily and looked away. She didn't know how to respond to her father's question, and it was unnerving to sit there under his inquisitive gaze. She wanted to shout out loud and say,

"Yes! Someone saw it and that someone happens to be my best friend!" — or rather "was my best friend." Laura and Nix had said nothing to each other since their late night telephone conversation. It was the longest they had gone without talking all year. Even when Nix and her family had been away in the Caribbean at Christmas, the two girls had still e-mailed on a daily basis. Now the lines of communication had gone silent and cold.

At school, Laura avoided her friend, taking the long way around staircases and hallways so she wouldn't accidentally bump into Nix between classes. She ate her lunch with Adam and tried to steer the conversation away from Nix and the events in the cemetery.

"I say she's guilty," Adam had declared the next day when he plunked himself down next to Laura in the cafeteria.

"Be quiet!" Laura responded harshly, but backed down as soon as she saw Adam's hurt expression. "Sorry. I'm just swamped; homework, my Bat Mitzvah, Sara's diary — and now this cemetery thing. I'd rather not talk about Nix, okay?"

Adam had shrugged and turned back to his lunch. But while she might not have been talking about recent events with anyone, Laura certainly couldn't stop thinking about them — day and night. And it had gotten even worse after reading Sara's last entry — the roundup of her friend, Deena, and others for deportation from the ghetto. Laura had had two more dreams the night before. One was about being a freedom fighter; Laura was crawling on her belly, through a darkened tunnel, a gun in her hand, when she woke up in a twisted mess of sheets and blankets. When she finally fell back asleep, she dreamed that she and Adam and Nix were on a train heading for some terrible unknown destination. That dream was even more terrifying than the first.

The next day, Laura decided to pay Mrs. Mandelcorn a visit. Perhaps she could talk to this woman in a way that she couldn't yet bring herself to talk to her parents or Adam.

"So, what can I do for you, my dear? You sounded very unhappy on the telephone." Once again, Mrs. Mandelcorn had kept Laura waiting in the living room when she first arrived at the apartment. But now, the elderly lady took a deep breath and settled back on the sofa.

Where to begin? There was so much that Laura wanted to ask about — the diary, Sara's life, the vandalism in the cemetery, Nix. Taking a deep breath, Laura finally plunged forward. "I'm reading about Deena's deportation from the ghetto. It must have been horrible for Sara to see her friend go like that."

Once more, a cloud passed across Mrs. Mandelcorn's eyes. She sat heavily, breathing deeply as if she were moving into a trance, transported to another time and place. And then, slowly she began to talk, filling in some pieces of history for Laura. "Those roundups took place in the summer of 1942. Each day, thousands of Jewish men, women, and children were marched to the train station at Umschlagplatz, loaded onto boxcars, and sent to Treblinka. Have you heard of this concentration camp, Laura?"

"I've heard of it, but I don't know very much."

"It was one of the worst of the death camps, about one hundred kilometers northwest of Warsaw. There were two camps there; Treblinka I, a forced labor camp, and Treblinka II, the location of the gas chambers."

Laura knew about the gas chambers. She shuddered to think how millions of Jews had been killed.

"The path from Camp I to Camp II was called *Himmelstrasse*," Mrs. Mandelcorn continued.

"What does that mean?" asked Laura.

Men, women, and children boarded trains destined for Treblinka.

Mrs. Mandelcorn laughed bitterly. "*The Road to Heaven,*" she said. "That's what the Nazis called it. Of course, it was really a path that led to death." Laura was transfixed by what she was hearing. Even Mrs. Mandelcorn's accent had become irrelevant, moving into the background where it was hardly noticeable.

"Can you imagine this, Laura? The Nazis decorated the entrance to Treblinka to look like a train station. There was a train schedule posted on the wall listing arrivals and departures. There were posters everywhere of places to visit. There was even a large clock that was set for the next arrival."

The Nazis decorated the entrance to
Treblinka to look like a normal train station.

"Why would they do that?" Laura interjected.

Mrs. Mandelcorn shrugged. "All part of the Nazi deception. The prisoners thought they were meeting other family members there. They didn't suspect that they were about to be killed."

At that, Mrs. Mandelcorn lowered her head, shaking it silently from side to side. When she finally looked up, there were tears glistening in her eyes. "Sometimes memories are a dangerous thing," she said. "Too many ghosts in the past."

"How do you know all of this?" Laura asked. "Were you there?"

Once again Mrs. Mandelcorn looked down. Laura sensed that she couldn't press the elderly woman any further, but her own head was pounding. There were so many questions; so many things she wanted to know. And one question echoed more than any other — what had happened to Deena and Sara? Somehow Laura couldn't bring herself to ask. She still had to finish the journal — she had one section left to go. But she was dreading the ending now more than ever.

"Most were killed in those transports," continued Mrs. Mandelcorn, more softly, as if she were reading Laura's mind. "So few survived." Then she shook her head. "Come, have another piece of cake. You are a little bird. Eat. Eat."

Laura sighed. Clearly Mrs. Mandelcorn didn't want to talk about the past anymore and neither did Laura. Instead, she steered the conversation to the events in the cemetery. "Doesn't it upset you that these things are happening now?"

Mrs. Mandelcorn nodded slowly. "This is a terrible thing that has happened. But you must remember, Laura, that we are living in a democratic country where such acts of anti-Semitism are not tolerated. This is not Nazi Germany or Poland where singling out Jews was acceptable, even the law. I trust the police here to find the people who did this and bring them to justice."

Well, they could find them a lot easier if they had help, thought Laura bitterly.

"But there's more, isn't there?" asked Mrs. Mandelcorn, eying Laura carefully. "Something else that troubles you?"

Laura squirmed uneasily. Was she about to betray Nix by telling this complete stranger what she knew of the vandalism? And was it betrayal if you were telling the truth? It was wrong of Nix to turn her back on the crime; of that, Laura was certain. And it was that truth that was pushing Laura to do something, to tell someone. There was something about Mrs. Mandelcorn that tugged at Laura. She trusted this woman — she couldn't explain why since she barely knew her. And yet, an important connection was there.

"I have a friend," began Laura cautiously. "She thinks she might possibly know something about the vandalism. But she's too afraid to say anything."

"Ah, I see," said Mrs. Mandelcorn, nodding slowly.

Laura went on to explain that the culprits were known bullies in her school. "But my friend is totally wrong by not saying anything, isn't she? I mean, she's being a complete coward. She's only thinking about herself and not the victims here." Now that Laura was talking she couldn't stop her feelings from flowing. "My teacher at school once said that the Holocaust didn't happen in the gas chambers. By then it was too late. It happened with acts of discrimination just like this — one after another with no one doing anything about it."

"This is true," said Mrs. Mandelcorn. "There were not enough people who were willing to be witnesses in the face of Nazi threats to their own safety. I understand what fear can do."

"What would you do if you were me?" Laura asked quietly. "Would you also keep quiet or would you go to the police?" Laura had already imagined the scene in her mind, the chain of events that would unfold. She would tell on Nix, who would be forced to confess to the police, who would arrest the teenagers who had committed the crime. In the end, justice would be served. But would it be worth it? She would jeopardize her friendship with Nix and possibly her own safety. It was hard to know what to do.

Mrs. Mandelcorn reached over and placed her hand on Laura's arm. "I think this is a question you will have to answer for yourself."

Laura looked away. "It's the diary — Sara's journal. That's what's making me think so much." Sara's stories were compelling Laura to do something. After all, she was supposed to honor Sara's life through her own Bat Mitzvah. If she didn't do something with the information about the cemetery, then what did Sara's stories and her life really mean? There was only one answer here and Laura knew it.

Laura turned to face Mrs. Mandelcorn. "Did you ever have a Bat Mitzvah?"

Mrs. Mandelcorn shook her head and a soft smile crossed her lips. "No," she replied. "These things were not possible for girls like me."

"Would you like to come to mine? I mean, only if you really want to. But you've been so helpful and everything. You can bring someone if you want — your sister maybe?"

This time, a large smile lit up Mrs. Mandelcorn's face. "Thank you, my dear. It would be an honor."

Chapter Eleven

That night, Laura slept more soundly than she had in days. It was as if all the uncertainty, all the confusion of the last few days, had been washed away. Laura was clear about what she had to do. With or without Nix, Laura was going to have to tell the authorities what she knew of the vandalism in the cemetery. The police would take over and, from there, the events would be out of her control. But she would take the first steps.

Before going to bed, Laura sent an e-mail to Nix telling her what she planned to do. She thought she owed that much to her friend. She thought long and hard about what she wanted to say. Mrs. Mandelcorn had reminded Laura that people get scared when they have to stand up in the face of a threat. "When faced with that kind of danger, people feel isolated — like they are all alone in the world," Mrs. Mandelcorn had said. So, more than anything, Laura wanted Nix to know that she wasn't alone.

Remember when we saw The Three Musketeers at school last year? Remember their motto? "All for one and one for all." There's strength in numbers, Nix. I'll always be your friend.

Then Laura pressed 'Send' and went to bed with a clear conscience.

The next morning, she took the long route to school again, passing by the cemetery. This time, the yellow tape was gone and there was no sign of the police. Workers were at the site of the vandalized gravestones, removing the broken slabs of rock and loading them onto trucks to be carted away. Soon, she knew, they would be replaced with new stones and all the evidence of this crime would be gone. But would it disappear for the families of those who were buried there? Or would it disappear from the hearts and minds of other Jewish people in the neighborhood? A follow-up article in the newspaper had said that some members of the Jewish community were worried that similar acts would happen again. Sometimes you could treat a wound and people still felt pain on the inside. That hurt was much harder to heal.

As she approached the school, Laura could see some activity up ahead. Students were milling about, heads together, talking in small groups. There was a buzz all around the building.

"What's up?" Laura asked as several students she knew passed her.

"They caught them," one of the boys replied. "The guys who spray painted the gravestones."

Laura could not believe what she was hearing. There was a growing commotion behind her, and Laura whirled around just in time to see the police emerge from the back of the school. They were flanking three grade nine students, Steve Collins and his friends, Seth Miller and Matt Brigs, two officers to a boy. She pressed forward, elbowing her way through the crowd of students until she was close enough to see the boys' faces. Two of them, Steve and Matt were crying. Seth stared straight ahead, but looked shaken. Suddenly none of them looked particularly tough. They looked small and scared. As Laura and the others students watched, the boys were placed in the back of a police cruiser. The last image Laura had of them was all three boys with their heads down — and then the police car sped off.

"What stupid guys," said a boy standing next to Laura.

Laura stood dumbfounded until she finally spotted Adam in the midst of the crowd. He was hard to miss. Adam was wearing a tie-dyed T-shirt — bright neon circles against a fluorescent yellow background. He was practically glowing in the school yard. Laura grabbed him by the arm and dragged him over to a quiet corner where they could talk.

"Man, that was like something out of a movie," said Adam. "The police cuffed them and everything."

Laura nodded. "Hey," she looked up suddenly. "How did they get caught?"

Adam shrugged. "Someone saw them and reported it."

"Who?" asked Laura.

"It was me." Laura turned to see Nix coming toward them. Her face was pale, as if she had not slept in days. She walked slowly, with hesitation in her step. When she stopped in front of Laura and Adam, she looked around to see if others were listening, then took a deep breath, and began to talk. "I couldn't stay quiet about it. It was killing me — eating me up inside. So I decided I had to do something — even before I got your e-mail," she added staring at Laura. "I told my parents everything, and together we decided to come and meet with the principal. Mr. Garrett called the police and they came to arrest the guys."

Laura took one more second to take it all in and then she lunged at Nix, throwing her arms around her friend and squeezing with all her might.

"Hey, cut it out! You're going to suffocate me." Nix squirmed to get out of Laura's grasp. But when Laura stepped back she could see that Nix looked relieved and grateful for the affectionate show of support.

"Are you crying?" Nix asked.

Sure enough, tears were rolling down Laura's cheeks and she wasn't even trying to brush them away. "I'm so happy," Laura blubbered. "I knew you'd come through, Nix." Her friend had not let her down. In the end, everything Laura knew and believed about Nix was true. She had done the right thing.

"What are you wearing?" Nix turned to face Adam who was watching the exchange.

Adam smiled awkwardly and tugged at his bright T-shirt. "So, I don't get it," he said, turning to Laura. "Did you know something about this?"

Laura laughed between her tears. "I'll explain it to you later, Ad. I promise." She turned back to Nix who had grown quiet and serious.

"They say I'm some kind of hero for reporting it," Nix said. "But I don't feel like that. I mean, I'm glad that I did what I did. But I'm still kind of scared. I'm going to have to go to the courthouse, and maybe testify about what I saw."

"Don't worry," Laura sniffled. "We're here for you — always."

Nix eyed her two friends doubtfully. "Great!" she said. "I've got a peace-loving hippie and a crybaby to protect me. And you wonder why I don't feel safe?"

Adam smiled and threw his arm around Nix's shoulder. "'You either get tired fighting for peace, or you die.' That's a quote from . . ."

"I know," interrupted Nix. "John Lennon."

"Strength in numbers," gulped Laura as she smiled at her best friends.

Chapter
Twelve

Laura stared at the blank screen of her computer, wondering for the hundredth time how she was going to fill it with words. The Hebrew lessons for her Bat Mitzvah were now complete. She had learned all of the prayers she would need to recite during the special ceremony. The seating plan for the evening party was finished, clothing was bought, and all details taken care of. Laura's Bat Mitzvah was literally around the corner, only days away. The only thing left to do was write her speech. And that was proving to be a daunting task.

How am I ever going to honor Sara's life in a meaningful way? Laura wondered as she rested her head in her hands and closed her eyes. The events of the previous days flashed before her. The three boys who had vandalized the cemetery had apparently been involved in similar acts of vandalism around the city. That news had been all over the school within hours of their arrest. One of Laura's teachers suggested that the boys had not meant to offend Jewish people with their behavior — this was simply a prank that had gone too far. Laura wasn't sure she bought that. But perhaps she would never know why they had committed this crime. The important thing was they had been stopped. Laura's father said that they could be charged with criminal mischief and defacing public property, and might face jail time of up to one year. In all likelihood, they would receive parole and have to do some kind of community service. Maybe they'll have to clean up the Jewish cemeteries, thought Laura wryly. Now that would be justice!

There was talk that Nix was going to be given some kind of good citizenship award for reporting what she saw. The reaction to Nix around the school had been like nothing she could have imagined. Students she had never before talked to approached her with words of congratulations and admiration. Teachers stopped her to tell her how proud they were that she had come forward. Someone from the local newspaper even showed up to interview Nix, though Mr. Garrett had appeared out of nowhere and quickly ushered the reporters off school property. There was one incident; a couple of big grade nine students blocked Nix from walking into the lunchroom. They were about to say something when Adam pushed in front of Nix and stood nose to nose with one of the older boys. They faced off in front of one another, neither one moving a muscle, until the bigger boys just turned and walked away.

"Maybe the T-shirt scared them off," Adam had said. His voice had been a bit shaky despite his tough show. Laura had never felt prouder to have Nix and Adam as her best friends. Now if only she could write this speech.

"Laura, read to me!" Emma burst into Laura's room waving a book in the air — her favorite, *Where the Wild Things Are*. Every member of the family, including Laura, had probably read that book to Emma at least fifty times, if not more. Emma herself could recite it by heart. "That's because I am a wild thing," she often said proudly.

Normally, Laura would have turned on her little sister for entering her private domain without knocking. She would have screamed at Emma and then called her mother for backup. But not this time.

"Em, I'm really busy right now," said Laura calmly as her sister thrust the book into her face. "But I promise I will read to you when you're in bed. Will you call me when you're ready?"

Emma stopped, startled and puzzled by the gentle response from her sister. She glanced at the journal on Laura's desk and then looked up. "What's that?" she asked.

Laura paused, and then replied, "It's a story. It was written by a girl my age. I'm reading it for my Bat Mitzvah."

Emma nodded. "Is it a sad story?"

How did she know? Laura wondered before nodding her head. "A little."

Emma looked thoughtful. "I don't like sad stories."

"Me neither." Laura laughed softly, reaching down to give Emma a quick hug before ushering her out.

Then she returned to her desk and stared once more at the blank computer screen. It was the diary — Sara's stories — and the incident in the cemetery that had changed Laura's perspective on so many things: family, friendship, tolerance. What was important was writing a speech that paid tribute to Sara's life and captured what Laura had learned from her and from these other events. Why couldn't she just write some words down and be done with it?

But in her heart, Laura knew there was something else that was preventing her from writing this speech, something that she was having difficulty facing, and that was the last part of the journal. There was still one section left to read, and Laura was dreading the end of the story. Deep down, she believed that Sara had not survived the war, and that belief was almost more than Laura could bear. She had avoided the diary for several days now; it was like avoiding the truth. Returning home from school that day, she had tried to pick it up, thinking the previous days' events had given her the strength she needed to read the ending. Laura read the first two short entries.

September 15, 1942

I miss Deena. Nothing more to say.

Sara Gittler

146

December 26, 1942
Another winter in the ghetto. Mama managed to find me on old coat. This one is so big and long, it touches the ground when I walk. But at least it's warm.

Sara Gittler

It was difficult to find a warm coat in the ghetto.

But then she stopped reading. And yet she knew there was no way that she could write this speech without first finishing the diary. That was the part she had to complete, and now was the time to do it. Laura picked up the book and moved over to her bed, staring again at the handwriting and the little drawings in the margin. Reluctantly, she turned to the last pages and, with a deep sigh, began to read.

January 5, 1943

And now it is happening to us. Yesterday, Tateh arrived home looking more distressed than I have ever seen him. Mama grabbed his arm as if she knew what was going on without his having to say a word. "What is it, Tateh?" I asked. At first, he wouldn't answer. He wouldn't even look at me. And his reaction, the fear and uncertainty in his eyes, was enough to send a chill through my body.

"We're being deported, that's what!" David stood sullenly in a corner of the room and spat these angry words out loud, breaking the terrifying silence.

Tateh still didn't speak, but Bubbeh started wailing and sobbing so loud that for a moment I almost forgot what David had said. I turned and put my arm around Bubbeh's shoulder, trying unsuccessfully to console her. But a moment later, I looked back at my father. "Is David right, Tateh? Are we being deported?" I almost choked on the word and a taste so vile rose in my throat that I thought I was going to throw up. I had to turn away to catch my breath. Tateh could only nod at me. No words came out of his mouth.

"I knew it," said David angrily. "I knew it was only a matter of time before it would happen to all of us. You think we're safe here just because we're behind these walls? Well, we're not. It's been happening to our friends and neighbors, and now it's our turn!"

"Stop, David," pleaded Mama. "You're scaring Sara."

My cheeks were burning as if a fever had suddenly and violently swept through my body. I heard a small moan behind me, and turned to see Hinda crouched in a corner. She was rocking back and forth and had covered her head with a small blanket as if she could somehow hide from what was happening. Mama approached me and tried to put her arms around me but I pushed her away. "You think I don't know what it means to be deported?" I shouted. "I'm not a baby, Mama. I watched Deena leave and the children from the orphanage. I know where we're

Jews waited at the train station to be taken to concentration camps.

going and I know what it means." I had heard David talking about the concentration camps further east. I had heard all the rumors from people on the street who spoke of the mass torture and killing of Jews in those places. There was no one who could hide from the truth.

"We don't know what will happen to us when we leave here," Tateh finally spoke, his voice loud and firm. "The fate of others is not necessarily our fate. You don't know everything there is to know, David."

David laughed bitterly. "You can try to fool yourself if you want," he said. "But I'm not so naïve." And with that, David turned and walked out of the apartment. For a moment no one spoke.

"When?" I finally asked.

"A few days," Tateh replied. "We've been given a bit of time, not like the ones who were rounded up with no notice." I knew he was talking about Deena and the others and I cringed. "We can prepare for this," Tateh continued. "We've been told to pack one small suitcase each. More hard decisions to make, Saraleh, about what to take and what to leave behind." He smiled fleetingly. "The important thing is that we are going together. We're still a family and no one is breaking us apart."

Tateh turned and disappeared into his bedroom with Mama. Hinda pulled herself off the floor and rushed after them. Bubbeh was still wailing softly and I took her by the shoulders and steered her into her small room. Then I returned to the kitchen. All alone, I sank down onto David's empty cot and grabbed his pillow, pushing it hard against my face so I wouldn't cry out. One thought kept running through my mind. I did not want to die! I was too young. In other places, girls my age were dreaming of dances and pretty clothes and vacations — not of the possibility of being killed. How was it possible that this was happening? And why us? What had Mama, or Tateh, or Hinda done? What had I done that was so wrong? I had never hurt anyone. I never hated other people just because of their religion, or the color of their hair or eyes. So why did so many people hate us — hate me? And why did they want us dead?

It was easy to point a finger at the Nazi soldiers who stood guard at the gates of the ghetto. It was simple to say that they were responsible for this prison. They, under that evil man, Adolf Hitler, were the ones who were trying to punish us for the crime of being Jewish. But where was everyone else? There were millions of people out there in countries around the world, witnesses to what was happening here. Why was no one coming to our rescue? That was even more difficult to understand. Did the whole world hate us too?

My brain was pounding with so many unanswerable questions. And finally, I laid my head on David's pillow, exhausted and weak. I needed to escape from all of this and in that moment my only escape was sleep.

Sara Gittler

January 7, 1943

When David announced that he wasn't going with us on the transport, I was not surprised. I had watched him, sullen and brooding, from the moment Tateh told us we were going to have to go. He would pace restlessly in the apartment, and then leave abruptly. He'd be gone for hours, longer than usual. And when he finally returned, he looked as if he was ready to explode.

In fact, when he finally blurted out that he was going to stay in the ghetto and defy the deportation order, no one seemed surprised, not even my parents. "What will you do, David?" asked Tateh. In the last day, Tateh had become almost shriveled. His tall body was bent over. His eyes were sunken and his skin was so pale it was as if the blood in his body had disappeared.

"I'm going to stay and fight," David said. "There are groups of us, all over the ghetto. We're not going to give in to them. We've got guns and we've got ammunition."

Tateh nodded. "I see," he said softly. "And you think with a few guns you can stand up to the Nazi army?"

"We know these streets and buildings better than any Nazi does. That's our advantage. That, and the element of surprise. They don't expect us to resist."

Tateh nodded again and opened his mouth as if he were going to speak. Then he stopped. I think right then and there, he lost his will to argue with David. That's when Mama stepped in.

"Where will you live? How will you eat?" she asked.

David shrugged his shoulders. "Don't worry about those things, Mama," he said. "You worry about yourselves. I'll be fine."

And with that, David turned and walked out of the apartment. This time, I followed him. I knew what David was doing by staying back, and I understood why. But I needed to talk to him. I caught up with him on the steps of the building and when he saw the look on my face, he grabbed me by my arm and pulled me into the courtyard. There, in the shadow of the building, we sank down onto the ground facing one another. At first, neither one of us spoke. But it wasn't that angry kind of silence that was typical of how David was with everyone. This time, it was a quiet filled with the struggle to understand what was going to happen to all of us. Finally, David broke the silence.

"I won't walk to my death," he said. "Even if it means I have to abandon you and the family."

I nodded and waited until David spoke again.

"There are more and more of us who are in the resistance, Sara. They are determined to fight back. Mordechai Anielewicz — he's the leader and he's only twenty-three, just a few years older than I am. He's been organizing underground activities here in the ghetto for months, bringing together different groups into what he calls the Jewish Fighting Organization. That's our name. And Mordechai isn't the only one. There are others; Aharon Bruskin, Mira Fuchrer, David Hochberg, Leah Perlstein." It was the first time that David had named the leaders of the resistance group and I listened in awe as he talked openly about their activities. I had continued to run messages for David for months now, trusting him, asking few questions, handing over letters and small packages, and just believing that I was doing some good. But now David was putting all of the pieces together. "I know that we have the means to fight and to fight hard," continued David. "We'll teach a lesson to these Nazis that Jews can stand up for themselves. We'll show them that we are strong. And even if we die in this battle, then I'd rather die here."

David's eyes were shining and he spoke with more excitement and certainty than I had heard in a long time. I couldn't argue with him. I couldn't beg him to come with us on the transport when deep in my heart, I envied him his passion. I couldn't avoid thinking about the possibility that the transports would be taking us to our death. And while David faced the danger of being killed here in the ghetto, maybe staying and fighting was the better alternative. At least fighting would make you feel as if you were doing something — standing up for yourself.

Young men and women were part of the Jewish resistance.

Mordechai Anielewicz (far right) was the leader of the Jewish Fighting Organization.

154

What an impossible choice to have to make, I thought. Go with my family and face death, or stay and fight and face death. No choice at all, really.

But in the end I knew that even if I did want to stay with David, Mama and Tateh would never agree. And to be honest, I could never desert my parents. David could stay behind, but I had to be there for Hinda and for Bubbeh. That was where I needed to be, where I was needed most, no matter what.

Finally, I reached up and gave David a hug — the first and only hug I can remember. And I whispered in his ear, "Fight for me, too."

Sara Gittler

January 8, 1943

What am I going to do with all this writing? We've spent the last few days sorting through our belongings and deciding what to take on the journey. That is, Mama and I are doing the sorting. Bubbeh is still sitting in one place, crying. Tateh spends his time playing with Hinda, trying to distract her while Mama puts aside her last few toys in favor of the more essential items. Mind you, there is so little to sort through that the decisions are not that difficult. Take the coat, leave the chair. Take the blanket, leave the pot. It pretty much boils down to clothes and food over furniture and fixtures. Those are the easy decisions. But the harder ones have to do with personal things, like photographs and my writing.

Here's the thing. If I take my writing with me, how will I keep it safe when I'm not even sure if I will be safe? But if I leave it behind, where will I put it? To take it or to leave it — that's the problem I'm faced with.

Sara Gittler

January 9, 1943

Here's what I've decided to do. I am going to leave my writing behind. I am going to bury it in the courtyard of the apartment building along with the drawings that Deena gave me. Somehow, that feels like the right decision, the safer option.

What am I saying? Am I admitting that I don't think I'm going to get out of this alive, and that I don't want my writing to be destroyed along with me? Maybe that's part of it, even though it's so painful to write that down. Even as I stare at my page, I want to erase that last line, as if by crossing it out I can simply wipe it out as a possibility.

But oddly enough, I'm not afraid. I'm young and strong. I'm lucky to have my parents and my sister and grandmother with me. I have faced so much in the time that I have been here in the ghetto. And I need to stay strong to face whatever is going to happen.

But in the meantime, I am going to leave the writing here. I believe that one day someone will come along and dig it up. And I hope that someone will be me.

Sara Gittler

Chapter Thirteen

Rabbi Gardiner was talking, motioning for Laura to approach him on the podium of the synagogue. Laura exhaled slowly, picked up Sara's diary, gathered her notes, and made her way up the steps to stand next to the rabbi. Her stomach lurched and fluttered and she took a moment to calm the beating of her heart. But when she turned to face the large audience of people who had gathered for the service to celebrate her Bat Mitzvah, all she saw was a sea of smiling, caring faces. She was instantly at ease.

In the front row, Laura's mother dabbed at the corner of her eyes with a tissue. Laura hadn't even begun to talk and already her mom was crying! That was no surprise. Her dad looked proud enough to burst. He beamed and winked, flashing a nervous smile in Laura's direction.

Her dad had been up that morning at the crack of dawn, scrambling around the house, racing from room to room, doing nothing except making everyone else nervous. It was Laura who had finally told him to stop pacing and go have breakfast; they would manage fine. When had she become so poised and confident? Emma smiled and smoothed out the pretty flowered dress she had personally chosen for this day. If you asked Emma, she believed this was *her* celebration, not Laura's. It was just like Emma to think she was the center of attention. But today, Laura didn't mind.

Laura took another minute to scan the audience: aunts, uncles, cousins, school and family friends. She was looking for Adam and Nix, and there they both were, sitting close to the front, each grinning from ear to ear. Adam wore a blue suit — probably the only one he owned. He looked pretty good, Laura had to admit, not the least bit as goofy as he usually looked, despite the trademark John Lennon tie Laura knew he had added just for her. She would make sure to grab a few dances with Adam at her party later that evening. He was going to love the music she had chosen for the dance. Nix waved discreetly, a show of encouragement, and Laura flashed a big smile in return. This was her moment and she wanted to take it all in.

A sudden movement at the side of the hall distracted Laura momentarily. As she turned her head, she saw Mrs. Mandelcorn making her way down the aisle of the synagogue, murmuring apologies to the congregants as she tried to find a seat. A slightly younger woman accompanied her. That must be her sister, thought Laura, noting the similarity in their faces. Late, as usual. But this time she didn't mind. Both women settled in their seats and looked up at Laura. She was pleased to see that Mrs. Mandelcorn had made it.

Laura was ready now. Clearly and confidently, she began to sing the Hebrew prayers that she had been practicing for months. Her voice was strong and had a sweet melodic quality that was pleasant to the ear. Using the silver pointer that the rabbi had handed her, she reached out to touch the Torah, the scroll of Hebrew scriptures that was rolled open to the section that was being read that day; she was suddenly stirred by the importance of what she was doing — this traditional ceremony of affirming her adulthood. Beside her, the rabbi squeezed her arm. She was doing well, and he was acknowledging her hard work. The service moved quickly from prayer to prayer and, finally, it was time for Laura's speech.

Opening her notebook, Laura once again gazed out at the smiling faces. She didn't remember what time it had been when she had finally finished reading Sara's stories a few nights before. Even though there were still unanswered questions, Laura had at last figured out what she was going to say in her speech. And when she had begun to write, the words flowed easily and she had finished quickly.

"I'm going to tell you about a young girl who lived during the time of World War II and the Holocaust," Laura began. "Her name is Sara Gittler."

With that introduction, Laura began to talk about Sara's life. She described Sara's family, her siblings, parents, and grandparents. She talked about the things Sara did before the war and then described how the Warsaw Ghetto had been built, enclosing Sara and thousands of other Jewish people behind prison walls.

"When Sara went into the ghetto, she had to leave behind most of the things she owned, everything that was important to her — her books, toys, pets, and many friends. She left behind her freedom and she entered a prison where she and her family had to live in a tiny one-bedroom apartment. She struggled every day; she had very little to eat, and almost nothing to do."

Laura opened the diary that Mrs. Mandelcorn had given her and read a section for the audience, speaking Sara's words aloud and giving them a voice in her service.

I dream of walking down a busy street and stopping in a café for ice cream and cake. I dream of going to a real school and sitting at the front of the classroom where I can listen to every word the teacher says. I dream of buying a new dress, or maybe ten of them. Most of all, I dream of being a famous writer and having everyone read my stories and remember my name.

"Those were Sara's dreams," Laura said, looking up at the congregation. "But I don't think she ever had the opportunity to make them happen. She and her family were deported to the Treblinka concentration camp. She left her writing behind, buried in the courtyard of her apartment building.

"When Sara wrote these words, she was thirteen and a half years old, just a little bit older than me," Laura said. "She had dark hair and brown eyes and freckles across the bridge of her nose, like I do. We both loved books and cared about our friends. Sara had a younger sister like I do. She once went to school, played sports, and listened to music. She even shopped for clothes and worried about whether or not she was popular. We were the same in so many ways. But when Sara thought about her future, she probably wasn't worrying about where her next family vacation was going to be, or which university she would one day attend. Sara worried about whether or not she would be alive. And when she wanted the world to notice her, it was not because she was stuck up, but because she felt abandoned, just like millions of other Jewish people at that time."

Laura paused and looked around. The audience was sitting in silence. Laura's mother wiped at her eyes again and reached for her husband's hand. Even Emma, usually restless and squirming, was still, listening carefully. Laura made a mental promise to talk more to Emma about Sara's life — to explain as much as she could to her little sister.

Searching the faces, Laura's gaze fell upon Mrs. Mandelcorn. At once, she was startled to see that Mrs. Mandelcorn had lowered her head and was sobbing noticeably, holding a white handkerchief to her face. Her sister's arm was around her shoulder. The two women sat close, heads touching. Laura was momentarily distracted and distraught. She wondered if she had offended Mrs. Mandelcorn in some way. But it was Mrs. Mandelcorn, after all, who had entrusted Laura with Sara's diary in the first place. Perhaps Laura should have conferred with the elderly woman about the speech she had planned to give. She had never meant to upset her in this way. But in the next moment, Mrs. Mandelcorn glanced up and gave a slight nod of her head. Laura knew that she was doing the right thing; Mrs. Mandelcorn was encouraging her to continue.

"I want to tell you about something that happened at my school a couple of weeks ago." It was then that Laura began to talk about the incident in the cemetery and how it had affected her at a time when she was reading Sara's stories. "It's easy for any one of us to sit back when bullying or vandalism takes place. We turn away and pretend it has nothing to do with us. We can even be frightened into doing and saying nothing when our community or our friends are threatened. During World War II, there were not enough people in the world who were willing to stand up for Sara and so many others. But reading Sara's diary makes me understand that we all have a responsibility to speak up, even when it is scary." At that, Laura looked up again and met Nix's eyes. Nix gave Laura a quick thumbs up and a reassuring nod before Laura continued.

"There are so many things I have learned from this incident in our community, and from Sara's stories. I have learned never to take my life and my freedoms for granted. I have learned that standing up for what is right is the most important thing you can do. I have learned about the importance of real friendship.

"We all know the terrible statistics; one and a half million Jewish children did not survive the Holocaust. Those were one and a half million individual lives. Each one was important, just like Sara's.

"Over the last few weeks, I have struggled with how to honor Sara through my Bat Mitzvah and I take this opportunity now to bring together the past and the present. My Bat Mitzvah day will forever be Sara Gittler's Bat Mitzvah day. Sara asked us to remember her, and by saying her name out loud here in this synagogue today, that is exactly what I am doing."

Chapter Fourteen

As soon as the service was over, Laura was instantly surrounded by members of the synagogue. Friends and strangers alike hugged her, kissed her, pinched both cheeks, and wished her *mazal tov*, the Hebrew expression of congratulations. She was pounded and pummeled from all sides, and she loved every minute of it.

Her mother had been the first to embrace her, still crying softly, and whispering in her ear how proud she was. Laura's dad was next. "You were great, kiddo," he said, his voice breaking. "Way better than I was at your age." Laura laughed before turning to hug Emma.

"Was that the sad story?" Emma asked, pulling away to stare into Laura's eyes.

"That was part of it."

Emma nodded and then hugged Laura again.

"But now it's time for your party," said Laura. "You did great today." Emma beamed and danced off, twirling to show her dress as she went.

Laura searched the crowd. Where on earth were Adam and Nix? she wondered. She was desperate to find her friends when someone spun her around and grabbed her in the biggest bear hug. It was Adam. "You were fantastic!" he said.

"Thanks." Laura returned the hug warmly.

"I told you this whole thing was going to be worthwhile," he added. "And now, we can party!"

Laura laughed and moved over to hug Nix. "I could never have done what you just did," Nix said admiringly. "You were great!" Laura didn't say a word; she didn't have to. The three of them stood in the understanding and comfortable silence that only good friends can share.

Just then, Laura spotted Mrs. Mandelcorn standing respectfully off to one side, watching the exchange with some hesitation. "You guys go on ahead to the luncheon," said Laura. "I just need to talk to someone. Save me a seat beside you," she added over her shoulder as she walked toward Mrs. Mandelcorn and reached out to shake her hand. "Thank you so much for coming," Laura said.

Mrs. Mandelcorn ignored the hand and gave Laura a warm hug. Then she wiped away the remaining tears from her eyes. "It's you I must thank," she said in a quivering voice. "I had not expected to be this emotional during your speech, my dear."

"I didn't mean to say anything that would upset you," Laura added hastily.

"No, no. I'm not upset, just moved — deeply moved," said Mrs. Mandelcorn.

Laura nodded. She was just about to ask Mrs. Mandelcorn to join her family and friends at the luncheon when Mrs. Mandelcorn's sister appeared. "Are you coming, Sara?"

Mrs. Mandelcorn nodded. "Yes, Hinda. I'll be there in a moment. Will you get the car and wait for me, please?" Her sister nodded and moved off.

Sara? Hinda? Laura froze. Her mouth fell open and she felt her head begin to spin. She reached out and grabbed Mrs. Mandelcorn's arm as the realization of what had just happened began to sink in. "It's you, isn't it? You are Sara. It's your diary — your stories."

It was like seeing a ghost come to life before her eyes. Sara wasn't dead. Sara was alive and standing in front of her. How could Laura have been so naïve not to have seen the truth before this moment? All the clues had been there — Mrs. Mandelcorn's age, her reluctance to talk about her past, the fact that she lived with her younger sister. Why hadn't Laura paid attention to any of this? Had she been so caught up in her own life and her own issues that she had failed to notice the obvious?

Mrs. Mandelcorn was smiling and nodding. Tears glistened in her eyes once more and she reached up to dab at them with her lace handkerchief.

"Why didn't you tell me?" asked Laura. She still couldn't quite believe that Sara and Mrs. Mandelcorn were the same person.

Mrs. Mandelcorn shook her head. "I wanted the stories to speak for themselves."

"But I would have done something more — introduced you in the synagogue, at least."

"Oh, no," Mrs. Mandelcorn cried. "It has been hard enough for me to talk about these things with you. It would be impossible for me to be so public with my history."

Laura shook her head, trying to compose herself. "Will you tell me what happened?" she asked. "I have so many questions."

Mrs. Mandelcorn stared thoughtfully before replying. "This is a time for celebration, not sadness, my dear," she said.

Just then, Laura's mother appeared from around the corner. She stopped and smiled apologetically when she saw Mrs. Mandelcorn. "Laura, we're starting the luncheon. Everyone is waiting in the social hall."

"Mom, this is Mrs. Mandelcorn, the lady who lent me the diary." Laura was still dazed from her discovery of who this lady was. She couldn't even begin to explain all of this to her mother.

"It's a pleasure to meet you. The diary has had an enormous impact on my daughter," Laura's mother said. "I hope you are joining us for lunch."

Mrs. Mandelcorn shook her head. "Thank you for your invitation, but I think I must go. Your daughter was wonderful," she added.

Laura's mother was about to say something and then stopped and turned back to Laura. "Honey, you really must come now."

"You start, Mom," Laura replied. "I'll be there in a few minutes — I promise," she added as her mother nodded and walked away. Laura turned back to Mrs. Mandelcorn. "I have to know," she continued. "You have to tell me what happened to Sara . . . to you."

Mrs. Mandelcorn nodded slowly and began to talk, carefully selecting her words, and picking up the pieces of her life from the moment the journal had ended. "We left the ghetto the morning after I buried my diary, January 10, 1943. We walked in a long line toward the train station at Umschlagplatz. It was the saddest sight to see thousands of people walking toward the station — a miserable and ragtag group. I held onto my Bubbeh while my Mama and Tateh held Hinda between them. We all walked as slowly as we possibly could. Perhaps we thought we could slow the passage of time, delay the obvious for as long as it was possible."

As Mrs. Mandelcorn spoke, time seemed to move backward for Laura. She closed her eyes, imagining the years slipping away until it was as if a young Sara was standing in front of her — her friend, Sara, the young girl with whom she had been twinned and forever connected.

"Hours passed before we boarded the trains," Sara continued. "I won't even begin to describe the train ride. It was unbearable — conditions that no human being should have to endure; no food, no toilets, no air. But this was only the beginning. By then, Tateh had stopped talking, stopped trying to convince us that everything would be okay.

Even Bubbeh wasn't crying anymore. I think she was numb and as resigned to her fate as the rest of us.

"We arrived in Treblinka the next morning and were ordered off the trains. Horrible guards were screaming at us and waving rifles in our faces. They lined us up, and then quickly divided the line, arbitrarily moving people to the right or to the left. Tateh and Bubbeh were pushed to one side, away from Mama, Hinda, and me. It was the last time I ever saw them. Tateh was right, you know. As long as we had all been together, we had all been safe. But now, my family was being picked apart, one by one."

Mrs. Mandelcorn paused and wiped her eyes once more. Laura didn't even realize that she had reached out to hold the elderly woman's hands, gripping them, hanging on to each word, hardly daring to breathe. Listening to Mrs. Mandelcorn speak was like reading the final pages of Sara's diary, the ones that had never been written.

"I managed to stay with Mama and Hinda. How the Nazis overlooked a young girl of Hinda's age, I will never know. Most of the young ones were sent straight to their death. Hinda was only eight, but she was tall, almost as tall as me by then. Perhaps the guards thought she was older than she really was. Perhaps that was one piece of luck that we still had.

"We were only in Treblinka for a short time, though each day there, each hour, felt like a lifetime. Mama died one week after we arrived. I realized only later that she had already been ill in the ghetto — a chest infection that was never treated. Mama never once complained or let on that she was suffering. That was Mama — concerned for everyone's well-being except her own. She died in her sleep in the cold and damp barracks that we were forced to live in. And then it was just Hinda and me.

"Can you imagine, Laura? I was only thirteen years old, a child really, and responsible for the life of my little sister. That's when I knew that we had to get out of Treblinka. A few days later the Nazis asked for volunteers to go and work in a nearby factory. People worried about volunteering for things in the concentration camp; you never knew if you were volunteering to go to your death. But I took a chance and stepped forward with Hinda. We must have looked strong, because we were once again put on a train and, this time, taken to a munitions factory where we were put to work assembling missiles and other explosives for the Nazis. It was backbreaking and there were many times when I thought we would not survive. But at least we were inside and fed once a day. That's where we were when the war ended and we were liberated by the Russian army."

Mrs. Mandelcorn's voice trailed off to a whisper. There was silence in the entrance hall of the synagogue. Everyone had either left the building or gone to the luncheon to celebrate Laura's Bat Mitzvah. Her family was there waiting for her. Adam and Nix would probably wonder what was keeping her from the celebration. But Laura could still not tear herself away from Mrs. Mandelcorn. There were still some unanswered questions.

"What did you do?" Laura asked.

"We returned to Warsaw as soon as we could. It was the only thing we could think of, the only home we knew. There we found an aunt of ours who had also survived, and we moved in with her. Hinda and I were both so sick after so many months of being starved in the concentration camps. We needed time to regain our health. We also had to try and figure out what we were going to do with our lives. By then we knew that my Tateh and Bubbeh had been killed in the concentration camp. Someone told us they had seen them marched to the gas chambers with the first transport of people from the ghetto. I was desperate to find news of David. I wanted with all of my heart to believe that he was alive, but deep down, I did not have much hope. Most of the young Jewish fighters in the uprising were eventually killed. They simply did not have a chance against the Nazis with their weapons, ammunition, and tanks. I never learned what actually happened to David, but I will always believe that he died fighting, and he died free, just as he said he wanted. He was my hero."

Laura fought to hold back her own tears. But there was still more that she needed to know. "How did you get your stories back?" she asked.

"It was many months before I ventured into the ghetto to try and retrieve my stories," replied Mrs. Mandelcorn. "It was an eerie feeling to walk through those streets after the war had ended. Everything was a mess; bombed-out buildings, deep craters in the roads, and piles of debris everywhere. All I kept hoping was that I would find my diary. I was terrified that it might have been buried under some wreckage

The ghetto was in ruins by the end of the war.

and would be forever lost to me. Imagine my surprise when I came across the courtyard of our building and discovered that it was exactly as we had left it. I found the spot where I had buried the stories on my first try. As soon as I started to dig, I felt the diary along with Deena's sketches. Her drawing of the sun setting on a lake is framed and hanging in my living room today."

Laura gasped. She had seen that sketch, had been drawn to it on the first day she visited Mrs. Mandelcorn's apartment. "But what about Deena?" Laura asked softly. "Did you ever find out what happened to her?"

At that, Mrs. Mandelcorn finally smiled. "She survived. It was a miracle that anyone from that early transport lived. Her family was killed, but Deena managed to stay alive. She lives in New York City today, and yes, she did become a well-known artist. She has had many exhibitions of her art, and I have been there for all of them."

One more piece of the puzzle had been completed for Laura.

"I'm afraid that Poland at the end of the war was still not a friendly place for Jews," sighed Mrs. Mandelcorn. "I learned of an opportunity for Jewish orphans like Hinda and me to leave Europe for North America. We arrived here in 1947, and have been living here ever since. That's the end of the story."

Laura's mother appeared once more from around the corner. "Laura dear," she said. "You really must come now. All of your guests are waiting."

Laura nodded. "I'm coming, Mom. I'll be there in just a moment.

You're really welcome to stay for the luncheon, you know," she added turning back to Mrs. Mandelcorn once more. Laura felt weak and filled with a mixture of emotions. All her questions had been answered. All the pieces were in place. The end of Mrs. Mandelcorn's story — Sara's story — had been terribly sad in places, just as Laura had feared. But Sara had survived, along with Deena and Hinda. And knowing that gave Laura some peace of mind.

Mrs. Mandelcorn shook her head. "No, my dear. I really must go. Please don't look so sad," she added. "Today you have honored me more than you can imagine. But more than that, you have honored my parents, grandparents, and David."

"It doesn't seem like enough — not for everything you went through," said Laura.

Mrs. Mandelcorn reached up to touch Laura's face. "It's more than you can imagine."

Laura nodded and then reached into her bag to pull out the diary. She opened it once more and gazed thoughtfully at the handwriting. Those words now meant even more to her than they had before. "Here," Laura said, thrusting the journal forward. "You need to have this back so you can keep it safe."

Mrs. Mandelcorn eyed her diary carefully and then looked up at Laura. "I think you should keep it now."

"Oh no," protested Laura. "It's too valuable. I couldn't . . . "

"But I insist," said Mrs. Mandelcorn, gently pushing the diary back toward Laura. "You've done something for me today, Laura. You've brought me some peace that I never imagined I would have. And in return, I'd like to give you the diary. It will always remind you of me. It's yours to pass on one day," she added, "just as you have passed on my story today. That will be the best thing you can do for me."

Laura clutched the diary with both hands and hugged it close to her chest. "I promise I'll visit you," she said. "I'll never forget you."

"I'm glad," said Mrs. Mandelcorn. With that, she walked slowly out of the synagogue. Laura watched her leave, then turned to rejoin her family and friends.

Author's Note

In communities around the world, Jewish boys and girls celebrate their Bar Mitzvah (age thirteen for boys) and Bat Mitzvah (age twelve for girls). It is a time when Jewish children come of age and a time when they are required to follow the rules and traditions of the Jewish religion. Boys and girls may study for many months leading up to their Bar and Bat Mitzvahs. On the day of their ceremony, they go to the synagogue and are asked to recite prayers and blessings from the Torah — the scroll of Jewish teachings. This is an important event in the lives of Jewish children, and the ceremony is often followed by a celebration of some kind, with food, gifts, and festivities.

In recent years, in an attempt to make the Bar and Bat Mitzvah an even more meaningful experience, synagogues have encouraged young people to "share" their ceremony with a Jewish child who lived during World War II and the Holocaust. In most cases, these children did not survive the war. Of the six million Jewish people who died or were killed at that time, we know that at least one and a half million were children under the age of sixteen. In some cases, young people will "share" their coming of age with a living survivor of the Holocaust, one whose childhood was interrupted by the war and therefore never had the opportunity to have a Bar or Bat Mitzvah.

When a young person today shares their special ceremony with a child of the Holocaust, this is an opportunity for many of these lost children to be remembered and honored in a small way. This program has become known as the Twinning Program.

The characters in *The Diary of Laura's Twin* are fictitious. But there are many real historical elements to this story. The Warsaw Ghetto was a real place during World War II, the largest Jewish ghetto that was established by the Nazis. It was built by Jews in October 1940, and was completely closed off by November of that year. By this time, there were almost a half a million Jewish people there, imprisoned behind high walls in an area that measured only 3.3 square kilometers (1.3 square miles).

Life inside the ghetto was harsh; there was terrible overcrowding, little food, and disease. Thousands of people died from these conditions. Some Jews were able to find work. But under the watchful eye of their Nazi bosses, they found this work to be backbreaking and tedious.

Beginning in July 1942, the Nazis began to deport the Jews of the Warsaw Ghetto to the Treblinka concentration camp. Jews were rounded up and marched to Umschlagplatz, the central square. From there, they were loaded onto trains and sent to the death camp. More than 300,000 Jews were sent from the Warsaw Ghetto to Treblinka. Very few of those who were deported managed to survive.

Inside the ghetto, a number of Jewish men and women banded together in an attempt to fight back. They became known in Polish as the *Zydowska Organizacja Bojowa* (ZOB) or the Jewish Fighting Organization. Their commander was Mordechai Anielewicz. At the age of twenty-three, he worked with the ZOB inside the ghetto and coordinated with the Polish Underground to secure weapons and train the young Jewish fighters to resist further deportations.

Jewish resistance fighters lie in the Warsaw Ghetto
rubble as the their belongings are searched.

The rebellion of the Jewish fighters became known as the Warsaw Ghetto uprising, and it began on April 19, 1943. The Nazis expected that they would crush the Jewish revolt within days. They greatly outnumbered the resistance with their large army and superior weapons. But in fact, the uprising lasted for one whole month. The Jewish fighters would not surrender. Using crudely made grenades, a few rifles, and other handmade explosives, they managed to drive the Nazis back. Finally, the Nazis were compelled to burn down the ghetto in an attempt to rid it of any remaining resistance soldiers. Many months after the formal end of the uprising, there were still reports of Jewish fighters in hidden bunkers who continued to battle against Nazi soldiers.

The destroyed Warsaw Ghetto after the uprising.

Janusz Korczak was a Polish doctor and educator who was imprisoned in the ghetto and was the director of the orphanage there. He had been the director of the Jewish Orphanage in Poland before the war. It was then that he dreamed of opening an orphanage where Jewish and Catholic children would live together. This of course never happened. While inside the ghetto, there were several opportunities for Dr. Korczak to be smuggled out. But he refused to leave his children. On August

Janusz Korczak

6, 1942, the children of the orphanage, along with Dr. Korczak, were deported to the Treblinka concentration camp. Witnesses in the ghetto reported that the doctor and the children marched to the train station bravely and with quiet dignity.

Throughout his life, Dr. Korczak believed that there needed to be a declaration of children's rights in the world. Based on his teachings and his writings, the United Nations adopted the Convention on the Rights of the Child in 1989. These rights include the right a child has to receive love, the right to protection, the right to respect, the right to happiness, and many others. To date, more than 190 countries around the world have signed the United Nations Convention of the Rights of the Child. Thanks to Dr. Korczak, children's rights are being recognized and respected around the world.

Heroes of the
Warsaw Ghetto Uprising

There were approximately 1,000 Jewish fighters who took part in the uprising in the Warsaw Ghetto, led by a handful of commanders. These young men and women were inadequately trained, poorly armed, and badly outnumbered. Only a very few survived. All of the fighters in the Jewish resistance were heroes, refusing to surrender to the Nazis without a fight. These are short biographies of several of the leaders.

Mordechai Anielewicz

This young commander of the Warsaw Ghetto uprising was born in 1919 in a poor neighborhood of Warsaw. When he was just a teenager he became a part of a youth movement that worked to help Jews get out of Poland. He was arrested and imprisoned for these activities. Upon his release from jail, he returned to Warsaw and to the ghetto where he helped publish an underground newspaper and organized meetings about resistance. He even snuck out of the ghetto several times to visit friends and comrades in other ghettos. All of these activities were moving Mordechai in the direction of becoming a leader, and in November 1942, at the age of twenty-two, he was elected as chief commander of the Jewish Fighting Organization in the Warsaw Ghetto. He began to organize this group to fight back against the Nazis.

In April 19, 1943, on the eve of the Jewish holiday of Passover, when the Nazis began the last big deportation of Jews to the concentration camp from the Warsaw Ghetto, Mordechai and his resistance army struck. Despite the fact that they were badly outnumbered by the Nazi army, the Jewish fighters would not surrender. Many lost their lives in the battles that followed. Mordechai Anielewicz was killed on May 8 when Nazi troops stormed his headquarters. He was only twenty-four years old when he died.

There are some who would suggest that Mordechai and the others who were part of the uprising never really believed that they would survive. They knew it was hopeless to fight against a powerful and well-equipped Nazi army. Rather, Morchechai and the others fought back so that they could choose the kind of the death that they would have. In a final letter to his friend who was hiding outside the ghetto, Mordechai wrote: "*I feel that great things are happening and what we dared do is of great, enormous importance. . . . I am a witness to this grand heroic battle of the Jewish fighters.*"

Mira Fuchrer

Mira was also a born activist and, as a teenager, had been a member of a youth movement that believed that the freedom of Jewish people could be accomplished by moving to the land that was to become Israel. It was during this time that she met and fell in love with Mordechai Anielewicz. During the Warsaw Ghetto uprising, she fought alongside Mordechai and was also killed on May 8 when Nazi troops stormed the headquarters where they were fighting. She was only twenty-three when she died.

Leah Perlstein

As a young teacher, Leah was also part of a movement of young people who were preparing themselves to eventually move to the land that was to become Israel. In 1940 she was helping to organize a group of Jewish people to leave Slovakia when she was called upon to help in the resistance in the Warsaw Ghetto. She worked outside the walls of the ghetto, purchasing weapons and negotiating with the Polish underground for their help. She was killed by Nazi soldiers in January 1943.

Aharon Bruskin

There is little that is known about the early life of this young man who was born in 1918 at the end of World War I. What is known is that he, too, was active in the Jewish Fighting Organization of the Warsaw Ghetto, and fought alongside Mordechai Anielewicz during the uprising. On May 7, 1943, he and a group of fighters snuck through the sewers of the ghetto to try and get help from friends on the outside. As they were climbing out of a sewer pipe, they were ambushed by a group of Nazi soldiers. Aharon was killed in that ambush. He was only twenty-five.

David Hochberg

This courageous young man was just nineteen years old when he became commander of a battle group in the Warsaw Ghetto. His mother had forbidden him to join the Jewish Fighting Organization, but David defied her orders and became a member of the resistance. During the uprising, he was defending a bunker at Mila Street No. 29, where several hundred civilians were hiding. When the Nazis attacked, it was clear that everyone in the shelter was going to be killed. David gave up his weapons and blocked the narrow opening to the bunker with his own body. He was killed immediately, but while the Nazi soldiers were trying to remove his body from the small opening, the entire group of civilians who were hiding behind him managed to escape to safety.

zivia Lubetkin

Zivia was one of the founders and the only woman on the High Command of the Jewish Fighting Organization. Her name in Polish, *Cuwia,* was the code word for "Poland" in letters that were sent by resistance groups both inside and outside the Warsaw Ghetto. In the final days of the uprising, she led a group of fighters through the sewers of Warsaw and managed to escape. She was one of the few surviving fighters. After the war, Zivia became active in helping other Holocaust survivors leave Eastern Europe en route to the land that would become Israel. She herself went there in 1946 where she helped found the Ghetto Fighters' House museum, dedicated to the resistance fighters of the Warsaw Ghetto. She married Yitzhak Zukerman, also a member of the Jewish Fighting Organization in Warsaw. Zivia died in 1976.

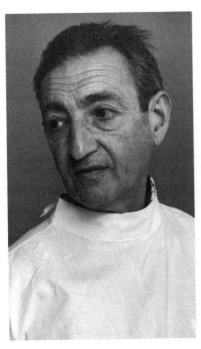

Marek Edelman

Born in 1922, Marek was only twenty-one when he fought alongside Mordechai Anielewicz in the uprising. He was one of three sub-commanders defending the brushmakers' area of the ghetto. Marek managed to escape from the ghetto in the final days of the uprising. After the war, he studied medicine and remained active in politics and fighting for rights and freedoms. In 1998, Marek was awarded the Order of the White Eagle, Poland's highest decoration.

The Memorial of the Heroes in the Warsaw Ghetto
Built by Nathan Rappaport in 1948, this monument is located in Warsaw on Zamenhofa Street where one of the main battles of the uprising was fought. Mordechai Anielewicz is pictured in the center, holding a hand grenade.

The Memorial of the Heroes in the Warsaw Ghetto

Real-life Twinning Stories

Gabrielle Selina Reingewirtz Samra
Montreal, 2007

It was a cool but sunny spring morning in April 2007 when twelve-year-old Gabby Samra faced an audience of four hundred friends, family members, and congregants who had gathered at her synagogue in Montreal to help celebrate her Bat Mitzvah. Not only was this the culmination of more than a year of work, learning and studying the Hebrew prayers and blessings she was about to recite, but Gabby had also spent the previous few months researching information about a young Jewish girl who had never had the opportunity to celebrate her Bat Mitzvah. This girl, like so many other Jewish children, had been killed during the war in Auschwitz, one of the worst of Adolf Hitler's death camps. Her name was Chaya Leah Dragun.

It was actually Gabby's mother who had the idea to have Gabby "twin" with a child of the Holocaust. Gabby's older brother, Mikey had celebrated his Bar Mitzvah a couple of years earlier, and he had also been part of a twinning program. When it came time for Gabby to begin to study for her Bat Mitzvah, it seemed natural that she too would find a way to honor and remember a Jewish child from the war.

Gabby's mother searched on a Holocaust database for a family who had come from the same town in Poland as her own father. She found the Dragun family and learned that Abraham Dragun had survived the war and now lived in Israel. Abraham became the important link to providing information about his family. Mikey, in his Bar Mitzvah, had honored Abraham's younger brother, Yitzhak Yaakov Dragun. Abraham's sister, Chaya Leah, became Gabby's twin for her Bat Mitzvah.

Gabby is slender and pale, with intense blue eyes and sandy blond hair. She is smart — attending a school for gifted students — and articulate. Though soft-spoken, she is strong spirited. Gabby never goes far without a book in her hands. But she is equally passionate about sports like soccer and basketball. Like Gabby, Chaya Leah Dragun was quiet, had long fair hair and blue eyes. She also loved to read and loved her friends and family. She was just about Gabby's age when the war broke out in 1939.

Chaya Leah was from Zuromin, a town located just sixty miles [96 km] from the city of Warsaw in Poland. When the war began, the

Nazis occupied Zuromin, and Chaya Leah and her family were sent to the Warsaw Ghetto. They lived there for three years, facing starvation, disease, and the constant fear of what would happen to them. In 1942, Chaya Leah and her family were sent to the Auschwitz concentration camp. She was immediately sent to the gas chambers.

Before her Bat Mitzvah, Gabby already knew a fair amount about the Holocaust, having studied it in grade six. She had completed a couple of projects, visited the Holocaust museum in her city, and had even tried to find some stories about children her age who had lived during that time. But learning about Chaya Leah through the twinning program was a chance for Gabby to form a personal connection with someone her age who came from her grandfather's hometown. It was like creating a bond between two families and two young girls, uniting the past and the present.

It is always difficult to find detailed information about children of the Holocaust. Unless family members were lucky enough to survive to carry the memories of their relatives forward, the stories of these children have been all but lost to history. Gabby was lucky to be able to connect with Chaya Leah's brother, Abraham, who filled in some of the missing pieces of Chaya Leah's life: what she looked like; what her interests were; how she lived before and during the war. Gabby spoke with Abraham and with his daughter. She wrote letters and put together a brochure that was circulated at her Bat Mitzvah, describing what she knew of Chaya Leah's life. Having a picture of the Dragun family to look at was an additional gift for Gabby. She was able to put a face to

Chaya Leah's name and her story. It created one more meaningful link to the history.

Still, there was much that Gabby was unable to uncover. Even today, Gabby wonders how Chaya Leah coped with knowing that she was facing her own death, how scared she was, and what she was thinking. These are details we will never know about the children who did not survive.

Despite this, Gabby was able to honor Chaya Leah in the most meaningful way. During her Bat Mitzvah speech, Gabby said the following:

When I think of Chaya Leah Dragun, the girl from Poland with whom I have twinned my Bat Mitzvah, I remember that this girl, and most of her family, died in the Holocaust because of the poison of anti-Semitism, a poison which was first spread by the repetition of hateful words. Of course anti-Semitism and the Shoah (Holocaust) involved much more than simple words, but evil acts often follow evil words. Just like many small snowflakes can become a dangerous avalanche, words can become bigger and deadlier . . ..

Sometimes the evil, like the avalanche, is unstoppable and innocent people like Chaya Leah suffer or even die. We have to be so careful about what we say and how we say it. My grandmother used to advise us, "If you can't say anything nice, don't say anything at all." I think that is a pretty good rule to adopt … Why don't we all try to follow it?

The Dragun Family

Chaya Leah is on the far left with her arm
around her younger brother, Yitzhak Yaakov.

Dexter Glied-Beliak
Toronto, 2005

"I am a grandchild of Holocaust survivors," said Dexter Glied-Beliak in his speech to the congregation during his Bar Mitzvah in 2005. It was February 26, ten days after Dexter had celebrated his real thirteenth birthday, and he was speaking in front of a packed audience of family and friends who had gathered at Beth Tzedek synagogue in Toronto. The weather had cooperated on that winter day; no snowstorms to interfere with the special event.

Dexter's Bar Mitzvah was made all the more important by the presence in the audience of his grandfather, Bill Glied. For his Bar Mitzvah, Dexter had chosen to honor and remember a child who had died during the Holocaust. And that child was his grandfather's sister, Aniko Glied.

Aniko was born on August 26, 1936 in Subotica, Yugoslavia (now Serbia). Her family called her Pippi; she was a gentle and quiet girl with a warm beautiful smile that lit up a room. She had long dark hair, which she would braid and wear in pigtails, held in place with big white bows. Like other children her age, Pippi played piano and went to a local public school. The Glied family of Subotica attended the large synagogue in the center of town. Of the 100,000 citizens of Subotica, approximately 6,000 were Jews, mostly wealthy families involved in farming or, like the Glieds, in the flour milling business. The wealth and freedom that these families had known quickly began to disappear in 1941 as the war was escalating. By 1944, all the Jews of Subotica had been moved to a ghetto, and shortly after that, they were all taken to Auschwitz concentration camp. Pippi and her mother were immediately sent to the gas chambers. Bill was one of only four hundred Jews of Subotica to survive.

He never spoke very much about his experiences during the war. Like many survivors, Bill found it too painful to talk about that time and what had happened to his family. At times, he even felt guilty that he had survived when his sister, parents, and so many others had perished. "I build a firewall around those memories," Bill said. He was particularly reluctant to share his history with his children and grandchildren.

It was Dexter's mother's idea to have her son participate in a twinning project for his Bar Mitzvah. As soon as she told Dexter about the idea, he was eager to do something. Dexter knew about the Holocaust; had learned a lot about it in school. And he had always been drawn to the stories that he had heard of survivors and victims of that time. But he didn't know much about his grandfather's history. And so began his journey to discover his grandfather's and Pippi's story.

Dexter began to meet with his grandfather, interviewing him about his life before and during the war, and learning what he could of his grandfather's little sister. The most difficult time was when Dexter learned about what had happened to Pippi after the family had been deported to Auschwitz. The last time his grandfather saw his sister was when they arrived in the death camp. When the doors to their cattle car were opened, his grandfather remembered seeing the blinding light of the morning sun. In the next moment, they were ordered off the train and were separated into lines. Pippi and her mother were sent to the right, and immediately to their death. "I never said good-bye to them," his grandfather said to Dexter. "I never saw them again."

Listening to his grandfather's story, Dexter was shocked and outraged. He himself has two younger brothers and one older sister, and couldn't imagine losing a member of his family in that way. "I am the age my grandfather was when this was happening to him," said Dexter. "It's so unfair to think that this could have happened." Dexter is tall and articulate, with a warm smile and dark curly hair. He is athletic and loves sports of all kinds: hockey, basketball, swimming, water skiing. But his true passion is music, and he listens to everything from classical to country. Dexter is the oldest grandson and has always been close to his grandfather; he even looks like him. But this experience of twinning with his grandfather's sister brought the two of them even closer. And a remarkable thing began to happen for Dexter's grandfather. As painful as it had always been for him to talk about his history, he found the twinning of his grandson and his little sister to be a joyous event. "With my grandson, there are voices now to carry my story forward," he said.

Dexter echoes that sentiment. He ended his speech in the synagogue by saying, "In celebrating my Bar Mitzvah I chose to honor someone who died in the Holocaust because I feel it is my duty to never forget."

Aniko (Pippi) Glied
August 26, 1936-May 1944

Acknowledgments

Several years ago, Margie Wolfe of Second Story Press gave me the idea for this book. She had watched a twinning ceremony while attending a Bat Mitzvah, and thought this would make a wonderful premise for a novel. That idea was truly a gift, and for that, and so many other reasons, I am grateful to Margie. She has been a wonderful mentor and friend throughout my writing career. I have thanked her many times in the past, but this gives me one more opportunity to express my gratitude for all that she has done.

Peter Carver added his experienced editorial eye to this project, and for that I am most grateful. His feedback was insightful and sensitive, challenging me to think more carefully about this story and these characters. It's been a privilege to work with Peter and to have him as my editor.

Thanks to Carolyn Jackson for the additional editorial review, Melissa Kaita for her creative design, and to Emma Rodgers, Phuong Truong, Barbara Howson, the wonderful women of Second Story Press.

My deepest thanks to Gabby Samra, Dexter Glied-Beliak, and their families for sharing their real-life twinning stories. Special thanks to Bill Glied, Dexter's grandfather, for talking with me about his history.

I'm grateful to my friend, Marilyn Wise, for helping with the translation of the Yiddish song.

I have drawn information about the Warsaw Ghetto and the uprising from several sources. Primary amongst these is the book *Brave and Desperate: The Warsaw Ghetto Uprising* by Danny Dor, Ilan Kfir, and Chava Biran.

The Ontario Arts Council, Writers in Residence program generously provided financial support for this project.

I have a fabulous circle of personal friends, writer friends, and family friends. I thank them all for listening, caring, and encouraging me in every possible way.

Finally and always, I want to thank my wonderful family, my husband, Ian Epstein, and my children Gabi and Jake. The three of them read early drafts of this book, and provided valuable feedback as I struggled to create a meaningful story. I am grateful for their honesty, their laughter, and their love and I return all that and more.

Resources

Here are some references for readers who want more information about the Warsaw Ghetto.

http://www.ushmm.org
http://www.holocaustcentre.com
http://www.yadvashem.org

Mordechai Anielewicz: Hero of the Warsaw Ghetto Uprising, by Kerry P. Callahan, Rosen Publishing Group, 2001

Emmanuel Ringelbaum: Historian of the Warsaw Ghetto by Mark Beyer, Rosen Publishing Group, 2001

Child of the Warsaw Ghetto, by David A. Adler, illustrated by Karen Ritz, Holiday House Inc., 2000

Janusz Korczak's Children, by Gloria Spielman, illustrated by Matthew Archambault, Kar-Ben Publishing, 2007

Photo Credits

Cover photos: all courtesy The United States Holocaust Memorial Museum (USHMM)

page 33: USHMM

page 44: USHMM

page 63: Yad Vashem

page 72: USHMM

page 77: Yad Vashem

page 79: Yad Vashem

page 80: USHMM

page 83: USHMM

page 84: The Ghetto Fighters' House

page: 85: USHMM

page 88: USHMM

page 109: Beth Hatefutsoth, The Nahum Goldmann Museum of the Jewish Diaspora

page 111: USHMM

page 114: USHMM

page 119: USHMM

page 120: USHMM

page 126: USHMM

page 132: USHMM

page 133: David Shankbone

page 147: USHMM

page 149: USHMM

page 154: USHMM

page 172: USHMM

page 179: USHMM

page 180: USHMM

page 181: USHMM

page 182: Yad Vashem

page 184: The Ghetto Fighters' House

page 185: The Ghetto Fighters' House

page 186: Yad Vashem

page 187: Yad Vashem

page 188: Tevan Alexander

Twinning photos are courtesy the Dragun and Glied-Beliak familes